# LIGHT FROM HEAVEN DAILY DEVOTIONAL PRAYER STUDY GUIDE

## INCLUDING HISTORICAL FACTS AND SONGS OF PRAISES

# GRACE DOLA BALOGUN

Grace Dola Balogun

Grace Religious Books Publishing & Distributors, Inc. New York

Presented To:

___________________________________

From:

- - - - - - - - - - - - - - - - - - - - - - - - - - - - - - - - - - - - - - -

On The Occasion:

___________________________________

Contact Author at:

www.Gracereligiousbookspublishers.com

1-203-891-7122

*Light From Heaven Daily Devotional Prayer Study Guide,*
*Including Historical Facts and Songs of Praises*
By Grace Dola Balogun

Grace Religious Books Publishing & Distributors books may be ordered through booksellers or by contacting the publisher:

Grace Religious Books Publishing & Distributors, Inc. New York 248 Lombard Street 2nd  New Haven, CT 06513



The author of this book does not dispense medical advice or prescribe the use of any technique as for treatment for physical, emotional, or medical problems without the advice of a physician, either directly or indirectly. The intent of the author is only to offer information of a general nature to help you in your quest for emotional and spiritual well-being. In the event you use any of the information in this book for yourself, which is your constitutional right, the author and the publisher assume no responsibility for your actions.



Also available in
Soft Cover ISBN:  978-1-939415-90-5
Hard Cover ISBN: 978-1-939415-86-8

Library of Congress Control Number:  2020919744

Editing / Interior Book Design / Cover Design / Publishing Assistance:
by CBM Christian Book Editing
www.christian-book-editing.com

Printed in the United States of America

Grace Religious Books Publishing & Distributor, Inc. New York

*"Just as Moses lifted up the snake in the desert,
so the Son of Man Must be lifted up that everyone
who believes in him may have Eternal life."*

(John 3:4-5) NIV

*"Yet a time is coming and has now come when the true
worshipers will worship the Father in spirit and truth, for
they are the kind of worshipers the Father seeks."*

(John 4:23-24) NIV

# *DEDICATION*

I DEDICATE this Book – *Light from Heaven Daily Devotion Prayer Study Guidebook* to our Lord and Savior, Who gave us the model of prayer and teaches us how to pray by saying, "Our Father who art in heaven Hollowed be thy name, thy Kingdom come and thy will be done on earth as it is in heaven..." (Matthew 6: 7-15). During Jesus' earthly ministry, prayer and fasting were included, calling on the Father for everything He did and was about to do, *(See John 11:1-44).*

Jesus, Who is also our Great Intercessor and is seated in Heaven, lives, and reigns in the unity of the Holy Spirit. He is at the right hand of God the Father, praying for us the prayer that can never be uttered. He is the only one Who deserves the great glory of this book. This book is from Him, is for Him, and for the saving of the sinners and the lost, as well as all the people in this world. Those who will read this book will begin a new life in Him, and worship Him in Spirit and in truth.

# CONTENTS

# PREFACE

Prayer is life to all Christian believers.  Christians' prayer is multifaceted prayer.  As one of the things we do without ceasing is breathing; therefore, we are to pray also without ceasing just as we breathe without ceasing, or we die.  The believers' prayer life must be ceaseless and a continuous practice as a child of God; we must communicate with our heavenly Father *(1ˢᵗ Thessalonians 5:17-18)*. Therefore, we access our inheritance in God through prayer. Prayer is the altar where we put all our needs and problems in life in the hands of Almighty God the Father, the Son, and the Holy Spirit, as the Holy Trinity, forever One God.

The Daily Devotional Prayer Study Guide is the most important book that all believing Christians of Jesus Christ must own besides the Holy Bible.  This book will help readers to communicate openly with their hearts to our heavenly Father, Lord and Savior, our Redeemer King, the Lord of lords, King of kings, the God of gods in everyday of our lives.  Putting all our worries, sadness, sickness, needs, afflictions, and trials in His Holy Hands. The reading of Psalms will open our hearts as well, to an intimate relationship with God our Father, Son and the Holy Spirit from the Old Testament to the New Testament until He returns to this earth to set up His Kingdom in a New Heaven and a New Earth where righteousness dwells.  The Lord God Almighty and everlasting Father brought us to get close to Him through Jesus Christ, His only begotten Son - the Holy Scripture say: *"For God so loved the World that he gave His only begotten Son, that those who believe in him will not perish but have everlasting life,"* *(John 3:16).* By His great mercy we have been born again with a new living hope through the resurrection of our Lord Jesus Christ. We have to give praises and thankfulness through our Lord Jesus Christ, in whom all life dwells, to God the Father Almighty, as we sleep and wake up every day to a new life in Him. Our prayers must be holy, clear, and in the harmony with our spirit to the Spirit of God through the power of indwelling of the Holy Spirit. Believers' prayers must reach to heaven, if they pray with all their mind and hearts – *(2nd Chronicles 30:27).* The book of Acts, chapter 1:14; chapter 2:42, chapter 6:4; chapter 10:31; chapter 16:13; 1st Timothy chapter 2:8; 1st Corinthians chapter 14:14; Ephesians chapter 6:18; John chapter 17:9; *"You will keep in perfect peace him whose mind is steadfast, because he trusts in you,"* *(Isaiah 26:3 NIV).*

God Almighty, the Father promised that He will keep the mind of those who get close to Him, intimately in prayer and supplication, as well as reading of His Words, meditating on His Word, and remain faithful to Him in times of earthly troubles. Those who strive in daily prayer and keep their hearts and minds to the Lord in prayer, trusting and hoping in Him. Believers must place their trust in the Lord because He is their Rock of Salvation who endures forever. He is our sure and firm foundation. Jesus Christ came to this world as the Prince of Peace, He becomes part of our lives in order to experience peace that He bequeaths, so that we might be united with Him in active faith and prayer.

Prayer becomes integral to help all believers to work in obedience to Christ's commandments, in order to live in peace; when we do these things, we are justified through faith, and we have the power of the Holy Spirit which dwells in us from this earth to heaven. Living without prayer is living without grace; we must humble ourselves when we pray.  We must not be proud and vain- but gracious in prayer.  Those who are proud choose to pray at the corner of the street.  They are making a public show of themselves, wanting people to admire and applaud them.  Isaac went to the field to pray, *(Genesis 14:63).*  Our Lord Jesus Christ always went to the Mount Olives to pray.  Peter went to the house-top.  Pharisees prayed to men rather than to God.  Believers must pray to God, as our Father who hears in secret and answers graciously, inclined to have pity, help us, and care for us.  He will reward us openly.  Our Father knows what we need before we kneel down to pray. *(Matthew 6:6-15)* We must also end our prayer with "Amen!" - Amen means that it shall be so; our amen is a summary of our hearts' desires.  Prayer includes praising, thankfulness, songs of praises, shouts for joy. Psalms 98:4 mentions making prayer with musical instruments and the making of melody - Psalms 46:2 gives dancing and an example of Jesus Christ triumphant entry with palm branches.

Mathew 21:1-11 speaks of believers that must be committed themselves to praising the Lord - The Trinity Father, Son, and the Holy Spirit, Psalm 9:1.  Almost half of the book of Psalms is about praising and thankfulness, which all the creatures, both human and nature are called to praise God Almighty, to include the stars, moons, the Sun, and all the planets, those in heaven and all the angels in heaven are called to give praises to God in whom  all blessings flow and from whom all life dwells.  Praises, singing, dancing is part of prayer to God.  When we pray, we put God to work and He will smile at us, and know that we trust Him. He also can do more, even abundantly more, than what we ask or desire.  We also put the entire heavenly host to work on our behalf like Daniel in the book of Daniel 10:13.  Angel Michael, one of the Archangels, came to help Daniel due to Daniel's prayer. Daniel received answer to his prayer because Angel Michael knocked down the devilish angel that was holding the answer and gave it to Daniel. Daniel praised the Holy and forever Living God. The same is still going on till today; the heavenly controls the earthly when we call on them in prayer.

# CHAPTER ONE

## THE NAMES OF GOD

In order to be able to pray aright, every believer of Jesus Christ must be able to pray properly; it is very important to know the Names of God, the Creator of heaven, Earth and Sea, and everything that dwells in it.  From the Old Testament to the New Testament, if you wanted to maintain an intimate relationship with someone you must know their name.  It is the same thing with God. We humans want to be a child of God, a friend of God, a servant of God, a follower of God; a believer in Christ Jesus, therefore, we must learn how to know Him and get close to Him intimately. Christianity is not a religion; it is a relationship with God.  We must call unto him by using all His Names from the Old Testament to the New Testament.  The songwriter says, "I am a child of God, He calls me friend." here are some names of God which we need to know and call unto Him in our daily prayers:  God the Father, God the Son, God the Holy Spirit; the Alpha and Omega, the beginning and the end. The First and the Last, the Wonderful Counselor, the Almighty God, the Prince of peace, our Savior and our great Redeemer, the Kings of kings, the God of gods, the Lord of lords, the Mediator of a New Covenant,  Advocate of a New Covenant, the Immortal, the Invisible, the only wise God, the true Son of God, the ascended Lord, crucified Lord, our risen Lord, the One and only that is seated at the right hand of God, Who lives and reigns with the unity of the Holy Spirit, the Father, the Son and the Holy Spirit, as One God forever. He is the Holy Trinity, the Holy God, the Ascended Lord, The Holy God, the Incarnate Begotten Son of God whom all life dwells, forever living, our Everlasting Lord, the Light of the world and the Life of the world.  The One Who was, Who Is, and Is to Come, the Almighty God, Powerful, Merciful God, the Counselor, The True and Holy God, full of truth and righteousness, The Wonderful Savior, The Prince of Peace, The Eternal Rock of Ages, The King of Glory, The Almighty God, The Lord of Hosts, The Lilly of the Valley, The Great Healer, Deliverer, The Provider, The Creator, The Potter, The Day Star, The Omnipotent Reigns, The Cornerstone, the Prophet of the Prophets; The I am that I am, The Great I am, The Savior, The Wisdom of God, Head of the Church, the Chief Cornerstone.  The Righteous Judge, The Protector, the Rock of Offence, Our Shield, and Deliverer, Merciful and Mighty God, Gracious God Truthful and Holy God, The Giver of Life, Victorious in Holiness, The Consuming Fire, El Elyon, Jehovah Jireh, Jehovah Rohi, Jehovah Raphael, Jehovah Elgibor, Jehovah Shamah, Jehovah Shalom, El Olam, Our Defender, Our Redeemer, Comforter, Trinity, in Council, Instructor, our Teacher, Our Provider, Inspirer, Reminder, The Invisible God,  Our Hope of Glory,  The Lion of Judah, The Root of Jesse, Man of War, The Lamb of God, The Sustainer, Convincer, The Light of the World, The True Light, Light that shines and no darkness can comprehend it.  The Restorer, Silencer, The one Stiller of Storms, The Proclaimer, The Reconciler of God, Father of the Fatherless, The Bread of Life, The husband of Widow, The Smith of Heaven, The Way, The Truth, and The Life, The Bread Winner, Champion of Champions, Winner of the Winners, The Composer, The Author and Finisher of our faith, Glorious in Holiness,  Fearful in Praises, Sleepless God, Ancient of

Days, ageless God, eternal God, Excellent God, Powerful God, Holy God, Leader of Leaders, The Chief inventor, The convener God, The Compassionate God, Commander in Chief of Heavenly Host, The Worthy King, The Overseer, The Boulder, Shaper, Breaker, The praise Worthy God, The helper, Richer than the Richest, Older than the Oldest, the Trustworthy God, Avenger, Arranger. Master Builder, Master Planner, Master Minder, Arrester, relentless God, Voice of Hope, our Hope of Glory, Beautiful God, Mighty God, Game Changer, our Refuge our Fortress, Our Buckler, Christ our Banner, Strong Tower, unchanging Changer, Unchangeable God. Incomprehensible, Incomparable, Unsearchable, Un-controllable God, Rose of Sharon, Our All in all, The Pillar of lives, The First Born, Lamb of God, The Glory and lifter of our Lives, The Word of God, Our Advocate, Our High Priest in Heaven, Bishop of our Souls, High and Lofty one, The Almighty, Our Best Friend, One and only one, The Almighty, Our One True God, Lion of Judah, Our Omnipotent, Omnipresent, Omniscience , Consuming Fire, Adonai, The Living Water, Unquenchable Fire, Awesome God, The Battle Stopper, The Unquestionable God, Jehovah Shikenic, Mighty in Battle, Glorious in Holiness, Mighty God of Valour, God of Miracle, Rock of Ages, Advocate, Amen and Hallelujah, The One Who gives the answer to prayers, Our Great Intercessor in Heaven, Our Interceptor, The Balm of Gilead, The one and only true Son of God, The one and only who was, who is, who is to come, Lord God Almighty, Father Son and Holy Spirit forever one God, Our Blessed Hope of Glory, Haaaaaaaaaaaallelujah!

May God Be the Glory, Great things He has done. He is the giver of a New Life and the Sustainer of the Universe. The Commander who reigns forever and ever. The One and only the Creator of all things, the Sustainer of all things in heaven and on earth.  The One whom all lives dwell. There is no one like Him.  To Him be the Glory and Honor Forever and Ever, the Holy Trinity Forever One God - Hallelujah, Hallelujah, Hallelujah, Amen, Amen, and Amen.

# THE NAMES OF GOD

# PART TWO

## THE NAMES OF GOD (PART TWO)

Lord, Our Lord, Our God, The Lord of lords, The God of gods, The Unquestionable, King of kings, The Almighty, Ancient of Days, God of the Elect, Unchanging King, God of Love, God Who brings Good Things, Same Yesterday, Same Today, Same Tomorrow, The Same Forever, The Ubiquitous God/Omnipresent, The Trinity, God The Father, God the Son, God The Holy Spirit, God of Abraham, God of Isaac, God Jacob, The Jealous God, God of the Fortunate, He that Act and Speak, He that Speaks and Acts, He that Talk and Do, He who Speaks and does not change His Words, He who Prophesied and comes to Pass, Covenant Keeping God, The Wonderful way Maker, The God of Spoken Word, The God Who Exalts His Word More Than His Name, Out Keeper, God Whose Barn is Full of Blessings, The God Who Blesses without asking for a reward, The Creator Who Never Forgets the Creatures, Great And Mighty, The Director of Heaven And Earth, Dependable God, Our Defender or Advocate, He that covers Himself with a Fire Branded Robe, He whose Sun and Moon are under His control, The God Who Gives Joy, God Who Puts End To Sorrow, God Who Fight For the Defenseless, The Great Warrior of Heaven, God with Long Saving Hands, The God of Hosts, Great Warrior, The Faithful Fearful God, The Most Dreadful by The Red Sea, God Who Commands The Storm, Peace Be still, Our Keeper, Our Guard, Our Deliverer, Our Savior,  God of Freedom, God of Forgiveness, God Who Delivers From the Hold of Sin,  God who pays our debts, The Price for Our Sins, The Resurrection Lord, Our Comforter, Our Lover God Who Has Predestined Us, The Victor, The Conqueror, Our Ever Defender, Defense In Time of War, God who parted the Red Sea, The Deliverer,  God Who parted the Jordan River, God Who Pulled down the Walls of Jericho, God Who Killed All the First Born of the Egyptians,  The Almighty God, Greater Than All the Earth, The God Who Created Lightening for the Rain.

We pray amiss, But He answers; God, Who Is Greater than herbs, The God Who Commands To Come, The God Who Commands to Go, The God Who Commands To Be, The God Who Can Close A Door And No Man Can Open,  The Unseen God But We Can Feel His Impact, The Invincible God, God Who Hears Prayers, Prayer Answering God, The God That You Can Call And He Will Answer, God that Answered by Fire, Creator, The First on The Earth, He Created The Heavens, He Who Established The Earth on Waters, Our Porter, He That Knows Us, The All Knowing God - Omniscience, God Who Does All Things - The Omnipotent, God Who Has All Things, He Makes the Heaven His Seat And The Earth His Foot Stool, He Who Causes Confusion In The Camp of The Enemy, The God That Spreads Out Across the Earth, The Great Hearer That Hears All Over The World,  Our Succor- Our Supporter, Merciful God, God Whose Mercies Endure Forever, The King of Peace, The Gracious God, The God of Love, The God That Gives Joy, The Comforter, The Blessed God, Miracle Worker, Wonderful God, Great God, Holy! Holy! Holy! Holy Hearted God, Immaculate God, The Glorious Trinity, The Truthful God, The Righteous God, The Life, Defender of The Truthful, The Light In Darkness, Mighty In Heaven And On the Earth, God Who Rescues From The Dungeon, Our Defense, The Trustworthy God, Our Confidant, Worthy To Walk With, Worthy to Associate With, The God You Can Call On, The Rock Of Ages, The Almighty God, Our Support And Defense, The God Our Rock, Our Shield, God Our Companion, Our Provider, The Lifter of Our Head, Our Help, God Our Hope, God on Earth, God In Heaven, The King From Whom kings Take Directives, The Silent Judge, The Just Judge,

The Just God, The King That Can Not Be Judged, Unquestionable God, The God Who Opens The Womb of The Barren, The Great Mother of Heaven, God Who Can Turn Bad Situations To Good, God Who Turns Bad Luck To Good Luck, God Who Sees the Visible and the Invisible, He Who Sees the Intent of The Heart of Man, The Great Adviser, Abba Father, Our Friend, Our Refugee, Our Protector, Our Healer, He Who Brings The Dead To Life, God of The Living, God Who Changes the Appointment with Death, God Who Has The keys To Our Existence, He Who Shuts And No One Can Open, He Who Opens And No One Can Close, The Un-searchable God, Fearful In Praise, God Who Is All Ears, Immortal God, Unfading God, The Kind That Neither Sleeps Nor Slumbers, The Great Worker of Good, Our Sponsor, Perfect God, The Good God, The God Who Goes About Doing Good, The Good Shepherd, The Living Bread, God Our Solicitor, The Beginning And The End - Alpha And Omega, The Living Door, The Goodness God, The Omnipresent God, The Greatest God, Our Redeemer, My God, God of Wisdom And Understanding, King of king, God of Valor, God of Life, Faithful God, God The Holy Trinity, Glorious God, God of Miracle, God of New Life.. Amen, Amen, Amen.

My God and my great Redeemer who lives forever more. The God of a New Heaven and a New Earth. All praises and thankfulness, adoration, glorification, magnification belongs to You forever and ever.

# SONGS OF PRAISES

*Holy, Holy, Holy! Lord God Almighty!*

*Early in the morning our song shall rise to Thee;*

*Holy, Holy, Holy! Merciful and Mighty!*

*God in three persons blessed Trinity!*

*Holy, Holy, Holy! All the saints adore thee.*

*Casting down their golden crowns around the glassy sea;*

*Cherubim and Seraphim falling down before three,*

*This wert, and art, and evermore shall be.*

*Holy, Holy, Holy! Lord God Almighty!*

*All thy works shall praise thy name,*

*In earth, and sky and sea;*

*Holy, Holy, Holy!  Merciful and mighty!*

*God in three persons blessed Trinity!*

*Holy, Holy, Holy, Though the darkness hide the*

*Though the eye of sinful man thy glory may not see.*

*Only thou art holy, there is none beside thee*

*Perfect in power, in love, and purity.*

(Hymn187)

# CHAPTER TWO

## THE WORD OF GOD

*In the beginning, was the word and the word was God. He was at the beginning with God. The Word became flesh and dwelt among us (John 1:1-2 NIV)* The meaning of the Word consists of God's revealing something about Himself through His spoken Word, which ultimately and perfectly personified His Son Jesus Christ. God saw the human condition, which is limited, fallen, and dependent on divine intervention for restoration and sustenance and designated His Son. The Word of God sustains the Universe from the beginning of creation, from the Old Testament to the New Testament, always, today, and forever.

The Word of God is the absolute uniqueness of our personal relationship with God the Father God the Son, and God the Holy Spirit. The Word of God is the means by which God created and sustains all things in heaven and on earth. *(Genesis 1:1)* God's supremacy is over all creation, whereas God Almighty has created all things by His spoken word. In order to maintain an intimate relationship with God, we must constantly stay in His Word. By the breath of His mouth, He spoke, and it came to be; He commanded and created and stands firm. His Word reigns supremely over all His creation. The Word of God unveils His creation which is transcendent and incomparable, and incomprehensible to His Deity. God's Word is an instrument of Divine relation to His people. God reveals Himself to all the prophets. They heard God calling them when they were sleeping, to include Ezekiel, Isaiah, Jeremiah. The quality of God's Word reveals God's love and His character; that is complete and all-sufficient, right and true, understandable, active, alive, all-powerful, and indestructible, supreme, eternal life-giving, wise and trustworthy. God's Word discloses God's plan for His creation. We receive the Word of God by Power of the Holy Spirit in our spirit, by the Spirit's indwelling in our hearts.

The Word of God will be fulfilled according to His divine plan for His creation; God's word is in perfect harmony with His will and with His plan for His creation. The Word of God must be obeyed, and demands human beings in the world a response that is harkened to, feared, praised, preserved, and proclaimed to the people in the world. The Word God gives new life, and sustains a peaceful life. It is living water bubbling welling up that nourishes creation from Spring on High.

The Word of God is Supremely authoritative for all creation. It is the supreme authority that is incontestable, unchangeable, irreversible, no power can erase the Word of God, and it never is void. The Word of God is a divine means of creation and meat of sustaining to all His creation, along with all things in heaven and on earth. The Word of God is sharper than any two-edge sword, and exposes what is hidden before God. The Word of God consummates the message of salvation to all the people in the world. The Gospel of Jesus Christ is the Word of God. Word of

Grace, Word of Christ, The Word of Truth, The Word of New Life in Christ, The Word of Reconciliation, - God was in His Son Jesus Christ reconciling the entire people of the world to Himself through the ministry of reconciliation. The Gospel must be preached to all the people in all the nations, to be believed and obeyed. The Gospel the living and enduring Word of Jesus Christ, the living Word of God and inseparable, supremely authoritative, reliable, sovereign, from a loving, Creator God that revealed the expected Messiah. Jesus Christ is the Word of God.

God's Word is supremely very powerful, able to create all this by His spoken Word, create the Universe out of nothing by His Word. Jesus Christ is the pre-incarnate Word of God; Jesus Christ healed and performed miracles by His Word, creating a new life out of nothing. Jesus Christ came in the flesh and dwelt among us. Jesus' Word is life-giving. What He speaks is from the Father. His Word will never pass away without being fulfilled. Jesus Christ granted eternal life to those who believed. Jesus Christ is the Word of life; He gave eternal life to the sinners, the lost, and those who believe in Him. Jesus Christ is the ultimate means through which God created, revealed, and personified Himself to creation. Jesus Christ has absolute and supreme authority over all creation. At the consummation, when Christ returns, His name will be "The Word of God" *(Rev. 19:13)*. The Holy Spirit inspires and empowers the Word of God's servants as they defend the Gospel and faith, as well as instruct and exhort believers in the world. The Word of God is all-natural expressed human reality was created, sustained redeemed, and will be consummated as the giver of life, what is given is unshakable, unchangeable, and unstoppable, will never be void *(Isaiah 55:11)*. God's Word is His creative power, and revelation that is perfect and all-sufficient. Scripture has revealed in His Son Jesus Christ the Savior of all the Lord of all. God revealed Himself in His Son Jesus Christ.  In Him, by Him and for Him and through Him (Jesus) all were created in heaven and on earth.  May God be the Glory! Great things He has done.

# SONGS OF PRAISES

*O Thou whom all goodness flows,*

*I lift my heart to thee;*

*In all my sorrows, conflict, woes,*

*Dear Lord, remember me.*

*When on my poor distressed heart*

*My sins lie heavily,*

*Thy pardon grant, new peace impart;*

*Dear Lord, remember me.*

*When trials sore obstruct my way,*

*And ills I cannot flee.*

*O let my strength be as my day;*

*Dear Lord, remember me.*

*If, for thy sake, upon my name*

*Shame and reproaches be,*

*All hail reproach, and welcome shame!*

*Dear Lord, remember me.*

*If worn with pain, disease, or grief*

*This feeble spirit be;*

*Grant patience, rest, and kind relief;*

*Dear Lord, remember me.*

*So that, when comes the hour of death,*

*My earthly fears may flee;*

*This song of praise be my last breath-*

*Thou wilt remember me.*

(Hymn 117)

# CHAPTER THREE

## FORGIVENESS OF GOD

In order to live a Christian life, and to be complete in Christ, every believer of the Gospel of God must have a mind and heart of forgiveness, as our Lord Jesus Christ forgives us our past, present, and future sins.  Forgiveness can be extended, forgiveness must begin from ourselves, in what we have done to ourselves in the past or present, within the individual in the family, and can be extended to nations.  God's Divine forgiveness and restoration of a relationship also requires the removal of guilt in our heart.  To forgive the offense of others against us is in order for one to receive God's holiness, and holy living.  God Almighty is merciful, slow to anger, full of truth, and righteousness, abounding in mercy, love, compassion, and graciousness.  He is the forgiver of sins; He never treats us according to our sins *(John4:2)*.  God's characterization as a merciful and righteous God will not leave sin unpunished; therefore, God's nature manifests itself in God's dealing with the individual and nations.

The book of Jonah states, *"God forgave the city of Nineveh, by sending Jonah to warn the city of their sins and impending judgment."*  The city of Nineveh believed, to include their King, and they repented of their evil way of life, violence, and destruction, as well as wickedness *(Jonah 3:1-9)*.  God, had mercy upon them and canceled the judgment against the City of Nineveh.  God the Father Almighty, holy and righteous, required obedience from individual people on Earth, and also commanded everyone to live a holy life, and to maintain a forgiving heart towards each other, thus He forgave their sins.

Jesus taught the Disciples how to pray in *Matthew 6:6; 7:12, "And Forgive us our trespasses as we forgive those who trespass against us."*  This passage teaches us that there are also sins that humans commit unintentionally *(Lev. 4:2).* There is also sin that human beings have committed intentionally for their own greediness, or because of the wickedness of heart; there is a recognition of the difference between intentional and unintentional sin, such is a violation of God's Commandments: Do not commit murder, steal, engage in fraudulent behavior against each other because of the love of money, sexual offenses, and forms of immoralities, immoral behavior, and disobedience to God's Law, whereby the person that sins intentionally, who sins in a defiant manner despises and violates the Word of the Lord, our Savior.  The worshiping of idols, the sacrificing and slaughtering of animals to idols, worship of the moon, rocks, mountains, ocean, instead of worshiping the Creator, who lives forever, are also sins.

Jesus Christ the true Son of God, the Lamb of God came down from heaven and reconciled humans back to God by sacrificing Himself, shedding His blood on the Calvary for our past, present, and future sins.  He saved humanity from sin and death. Christ offered repentance and forgiveness that brings forth spiritual transformation through His death, resurrection, and ascension with the great exaltation of Jesus Christ throughout the whole earth.  No one before Him and no one after; Christ gave all the people of this world the forgiveness of sins, resurrection of the body and life everlasting.  Jesus Christ opened the gate of heaven on the condition of repentance.  Christ required repentance as a condition of entrance into the Kingdom of heaven.  All believing Christians must have the heart of forgiveness and mind of forgiveness because Christ forgave *us of all our sins* and gave us a new spirit, a new heart, a new mind, a new name, and moreover a new life in Him.

# SONG OF PRAISES

*For all the saints who from their labors rest,*

*Who thee by faith before the world contest,*

*Thy name, O Jesus, be forever blest;*

*Alleluia!*

*Thou was their rock, their fortress, and their might;*

*Thou, Lord their captain in the well-fought fight;*

*Thou in the darkness dear one true light;*

*Alleluya!*

*O may thy solders, faithful, true, and Bold,*

*Fight as the saints who nobly fought of Old,*

*And win, with them, the victor's crown of gold:*

*Alleluya!*

*O blest communion fellowship divine!*

*We feebly struggle, they in glory shine!*

*Yet all are one in thee, for all are thine!*

*Alleluya!*

*And when the strife is fierce, the war- Fare long,*

*Steals on the ear the distant triumph-Song,*

*And hearts are brave again, and arms are strong:*

*Alleluya!*

*The golden evening brightens in the west;*

*Soon, soon to faithful warriors cometh rest;*

*Sweet is the calm of paradise the blest:*

*Alleluya!*

*But lo! There breaks a yet more glorious day:*

*The saints triumphant rise in bright array;*

*The King of Glory passes on his way:*

*Alleluya!*

*From earth's wide bounds, from ocean's farthest coast,*

*Through gates of pearl streams in the countless host,*

*Singing to Father, Son, and Holy Ghost:*

*Alleluya!*

*(Hymn 202)*

# CHAPTER FOUR

## LOVE OF GOD IN CHRIST JESUS

God is love. He has blessed all the people in this world with His unfailing love, unceasing love, and with His infinite love. The good Father Almighty has demonstrated His love in everything He has done. Apostle Paul stated in *1st Corinthians 13:13* and compares some of the fruits of the Spirit, such as that is in the Father, are hope and love. He and stated and concluded that the most important of all the fruits of the Spirit is love. God is Love, not only, or merely love, but HE is Love. God the Father loves the Son, the Son loves the Father, and He made His will known to Him. Our Lord Jesus Christ, in turn demonstrated His love to the Father, through His submission and obedience while He was on Earth. The Holy Scripture is the self-revelation of God's love, beginning from the Garden of Eden *(Genesis 2:17),* when Adam and Eve sinned, God demonstrated His love - He looks for them in the Garden; He called them and re-established His relationship with them. Adam and Eve hid from God after they committed the sin of disobedience. The Lord God made the garments of skin for the man and for his wife and clothed them *(Genesis 3:20-21).* God Who always loves us will not allow sin to stand between Him and His creature. God Almighty continues to seek us and the Scripture says, *"For God so loved the world that he sent his only begotten Son that those who believed in him will not perish but have everlasting life," (John 3:16).* God sent His Son to the world to rescue sinners to reconcile us to God and to provide them with eternal life *(Rom. 5:7-8).* Jesus Christ laid down His life for us, on the Calvary tree, on the Cross, our salvation is completed, the work of redemption finished because He is love. He does not want anyone to perish. He wants them to come to the knowledge of repentance and pray for forgiveness. The First Commandment for humanity is: "Love the Lord your God." We were unable to do so in the flesh, but in Christ Jesus we are born again of His Spirit *(John 3:3),* thus removing the old way of life and replacing it with a new life in Him. We die to a sinful life and resurrected to a new life, moving out of darkness to His marvelous light, this is when we truly love God and love our neighbor. God is the only source of love, with a new heart He gave us after we are born again, He is able to pour His love into our heart by the power of the Holy Spirit whom He has given us *(Rom. 5:5).* God's love through believers, made us branches who must abide in the Vine and continue with God's love. Only when we are truly in God's love as His children, He expects us to love, because whoever does not love, does not know God because God is love.

In the book of John, verse 21, He wants believers to keep themselves in God's love. We must love the Lord God with our whole heart, with our mind, soul, and with all of our strength *(Deuteronomy 6:5).* When we love God with our heart, we will be obedient to God and stay away from and renounce the world of sin and death system. We must love our neighbor as ourselves is a decision made to treat others with respect, for the safety of our neighbor on a level with which we love ourselves. It is a demand and practical working in our everyday life. The book of John says, "Dear Children, let us not love with words, or tongue but with actions and in truth." Believers must share with those who are in need of food, water, shelter, clothing, healing, we must demonstrate the love of Christ as our Lord gave us the parable of The good Samaritan *(Matthew 25:34-40)*. We must help those who are in need, even if by our word of comfort to anyone with a troubled heart. Love is the entrance to the motivation for evangelism. Jesus Christ's love commands and compels us to become an Ambassador for Jesus Christ, with the ministry of reconciliation *(2nd Corinthians 5:14)*. Abraham loved his son, Isaac, but when God called him to sacrifice Isaac, the love of God in Abraham was more than for Isaac; therefore, for the sake of the love of God, Abraham was willing to sacrifice the son that he loved without Knowing that God was testing Him concerning His love for Him *(Genesis 2:2)*. God stopped Abraham and blessed him more and more. Our Lord Jesus Christ, during His earthly ministry, stated, "*If anyone comes to me and does not hate his father and mother, his wife and children, his brothers and sisters ---yes, even his own life--he cannot be my disciple," (Luke 14:26)*. Yes. The word "hate" in this passage means love less. Jesus Christ demands that our loyalty to and love for Him be greater than every other thing we are attached to in the world, including ourselves; that is how the missionaries go into all the world for Christ. They do not care what can happens to them because they gave their life to Christ. Jesus Christ must be number one in our hearts and we must give to Him everything we are attached in our hearts to, to Him. He has the power to take care of our children, wife, husband, father, and mother, etc. That is why God told Abraham to sacrifice Isaac to Him; He wants to know that Abraham does not love Isaac more than Him.

# SONG OF PRAISES

*Alleluya, sing to Jesus.*

*His the scepter, his the throne;*

*Alleluya, his the triumph,*

*His the victory alone;*

*Hark! The songs of peaceful Sion*

*Thunder like a mighty flood;*

*Jesus, out of every nation,*

*Hath redeemed us by his blood,*

*Alleluya, not as orphans*

*Are we left in sorrow now;*

*Alleluya, he is near us,*

*Faith believes, nor questions how:*

*Though the cloud from sight received*

*Him*

*When the forty days were o'er;*

*Shalt our heats forget his promise,*

*I am with you evermore.*

*Alleluya, alleluya,*

*Glory be to God on high;*

*To the Father, and the Savior*

*Who has gained the victory;*

*Glory to the Holy Spirits;*

*Fount of love and sanctity;*

*Alleluya, alleluya,*

*To the Triune Majesty.*

*(Hymn260)*

# CHAPTER FIVE

## PERSEVERANCE

Christian believers must have the spirit of perseverance in order to be able to serve the Lord. Perseverance is referring to the idea of Christian living with the resistance of all worldly systems that can pollute the heart and mind of believers. Perseverance means believers' steadfastness under pressure, and endurance in time of trials and tribulations. Confidence in waiting on God's promise, with the power of expectation and in fullness of faith in God's words - Who is our Divine Deliverer, Who always delivers His children from any affliction, and trouble of life. Perseverance increases our hope in God's promise; it is profitable to the righteous in their lives, as they get close to the Lord every moment of their walk with the Lord. Abraham, Noah, and all the prophets persevered under temptations. In the New Testament, perseverance, faith, and hope are emphasized as the important fruit of the Holy Spirit. Believing Christians must be persevering in order to attain or gain personally the ultimate salvation of God.

Perseverance under suffering *(2nd Thessalonians 1:4),* Apostle Paul wrote boldly about the perseverance of believers because of their steadfastness *(1st Thessalonians 3:5)* of the Thessalonians under oppression during the Early Church. The

Thessalonians suffered persecution and trials from their own people, but they endured, tempted still - they persevered in faith.

Another example is Job's experience in the Old Testament that stands as an example of patience and perseverance. The Lord blessed Job more and more, rewarding Him for His perseverance. Our Lord Jesus Christ assures all the Christian believers that He sees and knows their perseverance *(Rev 2:2-3)*. Our Lord gave us the example of perseverance during His earthly ministry by His teaching of the parable of the sower - those who hear and produce a crop stand in contrast to the second and third types in the parable who fall away in time of trial and trouble of the world, because they were unable to remain constant, endure and persevere in adversity; they do not grow into maturity *(Luke 8:13-14)*. Therefore our Master's teaching of the parable of sower means to encourage believers to be able to persevere and produce fruit for eternal life.

Paul called Timothy to persevere with respect duties as a Deacon and Elder in the Church. In *1st Timothy 4:16*, he explains to him that his persevering will result in his personal reputation as a saved, born again Christian that will show the people to whom he ministers and preached, thus helping them attain the salvation that they will see the sign of confidence and perseverance in Him, and give their lives to Christ.

All Christian believers must set an example and practice what they preach, so that the people will see the character and Christian living in us and follow our example. By this they know and see that we as Christians are those that truly those who belong to Jesus Christ. Christians must develop perseverance. Perseverance must finish its work, so that we may be matured completely in Christ our Savior. Apostle James mentions the important addition which is the promise of God that says: "The Crown of Life" will be awarded to those who by their perseverance, show their love for God our Savior to the end *(James 1:12).* Those who persevered show their confidence in God's goodness and care, as God loves them. Apostle Peter in *2nd Peter* listed the qualities of a child of God and that Christian believers must develop in order to be spiritually victorious and fruitful before God. We must make every effort to demonstrate, must be actively involved in their Christian growth, just immediately after they gave their life to Christ, and strive to add to their faith (*See* the qualities listed because godly character does not automatically grow without our diligent effort to cultivate them): Goodness, and goodness, knowledge, and to knowledge, self-control, perseverance; and perseverance, godliness, and to godliness brotherly kindness and to brotherly kindness love *(1st Peter 5-8)* for if you possess these qualities in increasing measure, they will keep you from being ineffective and unproductive in your knowledge of our Lord Jesus Christ. Our participation in God's very nature is another description of the new birth by which we receive God's life. We share God's nature in order to be conforming to God's Holiness.

# SONG OF PRAISES

*Now thank we all our God*

*With heart ad hands and voices,*

*In whom his world rejoices;*

*Who from our mother's arms*

 *Hath blessed us on our way*

*With countless gifts of love,*

*And still is ours today.*

*O may this bounteous God*

*Through all our life be near us,*

*With ever joyful hearts*

*And blessed peace to sheer us,*

*And keep us in his grace,*

*And guide us when perplexed,*

*And free us from all ills*

*In this world and the next.*

*All praise and thanks to God*

*The Father now be given,*

 *The Son and him who reigns*

 *With them in highest heaven,*

*The one eternal God,*

46

*Whom earth and heaven adore;*

*For thus it was, is now,*

*And shall be evermore.*

*(Hymn 350)*

# CHAPTER SIX

## FAITH IN GOD

God the Father Almighty bestowed the gift of life by grace through faith in the gospel of Jesus Christ, His Son. He calls the Christian believers to grow into maturity of the nature of salvation. God's grace which continues to uphold all Christians believers, as well as enabling them to mature in their faith and be strengthened in the hope, which is the source of salvation, our Lord and Savior has prepared it as an inheritance for the believers who by patiently doing good, seek for glory and honor and immortality and to those who believe and have strong faith, and to those who continue and persist, God will give eternal life. *(Romans 2:7)* Faith, trust, and loyalty to a person, or in things, Christian believers will find the security and hope in God as revealed in Jesus Christ, which is a unique relationship to God in the Holy Spirit through a believer's love and obedience, as it was expressed in the lives of Christ's discipleship and in the service of Him. Faith is a fundamental idea of belief, trust, and loyalty in Christ Jesus our Lord and Savior. Individual's feeling of safety, and feeling of security in God, in himself or herself can become a faulty confidence; true security that our lives are secured in God, as a result of trusting, in relationship with God, obedience to God's Word and trust in the name of the Lord is in every area of our lives;

therefore, relying solely on His protection, where our soul finds rest in His Holy Hands. Believers acknowledge their dependence on God for all their needs and for protection during any earthly afflictions and trials. King David being pursued by his enemy asks God to save and deliver him *(Ps. 7:1).* Hope in God is an expression of faith. Christian believers must know that our God is a faithful God Who keeps His covenant of love to a thousand generations of those who love Him and keep His commands because the Word of God is God. Abraham has strong faith in God because God chose Him and sees that He is faithful; God enters into a covenant with Abraham. And resulted in recognition and acknowledgment of his relationship with God; accounted towards him and for him as righteousness.

Faith is a spiritual attitude involving activity. Abraham stood approved when he acknowledged the promise of God, and he trusted God's power to perform what He had promised: Abraham believed the Lord, and credited it to him as righteousness *(Genesis 15:6).* The Lord God indicated to Abraham His plan, and Abraham believed it, filed with a firm security in the Lord. Abraham's subsequent exercise if practiced and obedient actions are clear. These are indications of his strong faith in the Lord. In the New Testament understanding of faith involves an appreciation of continuity between the covenant of God from Old Testament to New Testament and the concepts of covenant, people of God, the revelation, and the activity of God, which continues from Old and New Testament that is defined by a new covenant where the people of God identified by their response to God's begotten Son Jesus Christ in a new language of the Gospel make it clear.

God is in His Son Jesus Christ and the Church where Christ is the Head of the Church, the Corner Stone, our Rock of Salvation. The New Testament expressed and defines what God has done, what He is doing, and what He will do in the future.

The meaning of faith is a reflection of God's continuity from the Old Testament and the expression of its uniqueness in a different setting. Old Testament faith means primarily confident to trust that which is based on God's promise as understood through the Word of God. *(Luke 1:20)* In New Testament, Jesus Christ is the living Word of God, and the Gospel message of truth *(Mark 1:15)*. In Jesus Christ, God is Father and King, this claim involves a unique sense of the presence and communion with God, as well as the call to His hearers to respond to His claim of Sonship *(Mark 12:1-12)*. Christ's interpretation of the Kingdom of God which the ministry begins with John the Baptist's, after his Baptism of Jesus in the Jordan River, experiences Jesus and the heavenly announcement of Jesus' Sonship *(Luke 3:22, Math 3:17)* The announcement was repeated to the apostles in the Mount of Transfiguration, which followed by God's command, "This is my beloved Son listen to him."

The result of faith is seen when people put their faith in Christ, they experience great changes in their lives. The Gospel makes the faith response explicit in particular miracles. Our Lord Jesus during His earthly ministry asserts, in a discussion of teaching that the power will always be available to all who have faith *(Mark11:23)*. Prayer is an important means of expressing our faith. Our Lord said if we have faith as little as a mustard seed, we can move a mountain *(Luke 17:6)*. To place one's faith and trust in Jesus Christ is to open the door for radical change in the meaning of life itself, which is a new life in Christ Jesus.

# SONG OF PRAISES

*All things bright and beautiful,*

*All creatures great and small,*

*All this wise and wonderful,*

*The Lord God made them all.*

*Each little flower that opens,*

*Each little bird that sings,*

*He made their glowing colors,*

*He made their tiny wings:*

*The cold wind in there winter,*

*The pleasant summer sun,*

*The ripe fruits in the garden,*

*He made them every one*

*The purple-headed mountain,*

*The river running by,*

*The sunset and the morning,*

*That brightens up the sky;*

*He gave us eyes to see them;*

*And lips that we might tell*

*How great is God Almighty,*

*Who has made all things well; (Hymn444)*

# CHAPTER SEVEN

## THE GOODNESS OF GOD

*"In the beginning God created everything good and therefore, without sin. After God had finished creating and was surveying what he had made he observed that it was good very Good." (Genesis 1:31)*

God's goodness never fails; it endures forever in the life of his people in all the earth, and under the earth, from the Old Testament to the New Testament God created heaven and earth all that He called good. God's goodness is bedrock of truth in the Holy Bible from the first page to the last page of the Holy Bible. God's goodness is expressed in all the book of Psalms by King David and others, to include the prophets *(Psalms 25:8; 34:8; 100:5)*. Jesus Christ affirmed the Father's goodness when preaching to the rich young ruler *(Matthew 19:17)*. Apostle Peter proclaimed the Word of God's goodness in *(Ps 34:8)*. "Taste and see that the Lord is good" God's Goodness according to the Holy Scripture appears very clearly in His dealings with His people. God is not only good in general, but He is good to me and you *(Ps 23-6; Luke 2:4)*. Humanity's goodness is an example of divine goodness; for human beings goodness is in service; goodness always involves a particular way of behaving.  Because God is good, He is good to His people, and when people are good, they behave decently toward each other, based on God's goodness to them.  Human beings' goodness involves right behavior, which expresses itself in kindness and other praiseworthy qualities, that includes avoiding evil, and which springs up from the inner being of a person.  The goodness of God's people shows itself in various moral qualities. These characteristic of behavior of good people, include pureness, purity, just, justice, righteousness, and "good" that shows in their daily living. Goodness involves not only right behavior but also avoiding all its opposite, which is evil and wickedness.  Christian believer's outward behavior comes from within.  In the same way, an evil person is evil from within.  Good people's behavior shows a good heart.  In the Old Testament, God's goodness to His people and their goodness is in response was based on the covenant relationship between them... God appeals to them as His people to return to the covenant relationship, which is called simple goodness, but in the New Testament goodness is one of the fruits of the Holy Spirit *(Galatian 5:22)*.  Where the moral excellences is one of the steps to virtue. As apostle Peter says: believers must make every effort to add to their faith goodness *(Genesis 1:4)*. God saw that the light was good - All the believers in the world must give thanks and praises to the Lord, for He is good, and His loving kindness endures forever.  We must exalt our God and King of righteousness, and praise His holy name from one generation to another because of the goodness of His protection, provisions, and all the great things He has done in our lives.  God is worthy of our praises and thankfulness because He is so good to us on this earth.  He opens the chambers of heaven and sends clean air to us; so that we may live and worship him in true holiness of heart.  God's goodness is incomparable, incomprehensible, and unsearchable, and uncontrollable. Great is His goodness in our lives.  We must shout to the Lord and worship Him with gladness.

# SONG OF PRAISES

*Lead us, heavenly Father, lead us*

*O'er the world's tempestuous sea;*

*Guard us, guide us, keep us, feed us,*

*For we have no help but thee;*

*Yet possessing every blessing*

*If our God our Father be,*

*Savor breathe forgiveness over us;*

*All our weakness thou dost know,*

*Thou didst tread this earth before us,*

*Thou didst feel its keenest woe;*

*Lone and dreary, faith and weary,*

*Through the dese thou didst go.*

*Spirit of our God, descending,*

*Fill our hearts with heavenly joy,*

*Love with every passion blending*

*Pleasure that can never cloy;*

*Thus provided, pardoned, guided,*

*Nothing can our peace destroy.*

*(Hymn 555)*

# CHAPTER EIGHT

## THE RIGHTEOUSNESS OF GOD IN CHRIST

The righteousness of God is from the beginning of creation to the present. God the Father is a righteous God full of truth and righteousness abounding in love and forgiveness. Jesus Christ, His Son is the righteous one; the Father through His only begotten incarnate Son of God and the Spirit gives the gift of righteousness to repentant sinners for salvation; such believing sinners are declared righteous by the Father through the Son, they are made righteous, washed and cleansed with the precious blood of Jesus Christ shed on the Cross for all the humans on earth and under the earth. The sinners are made righteous because they are in a covenant relationship with the living God, who is the God of all grace and mercy and who will bring to the completion what He has begun in our lives by declaring them righteous for Jesus Christ's sake.

The teaching of John the Baptist and Jesus Christ on righteousness from the Old Testament to the New Testament because in the Old Testament Yahweh Elohim, the Lord God is righteous in all that He did, spoke, and acts in accordance with His establishment of the covenant with His people *(Ps 22:31, 40: 1).* In the book of Micah, he declared that the righteousness of God is His faithfulness to keep and act within the covenant and to save the people of Israel from their enemies, as well as to vindicate the penitent.

All the people of God from the Old Testament to the New Testament are called to live righteously, that is, in the conformity to the demands of the covenant and according to God's will *(Ps1:4-6).* Living within the covenant relationship with God comes the gift of salvation, they are to behave as the people of the Holy God. People must live a holy life. John the Baptist calls for repentance and righteous behavior *(Luke 3:7-9).* Moreover, it was because of the demands of such righteousness, the fulfilling the will of God comes from, in the example of John actually being willing to baptize Jesus Christ. Likewise, Jesus Christ presents righteousness as conformity to the will of God the Father which was expressed in the Old Testament Law *(Matt 13:17; 23:29),* and as well also brought conformity to His own teaching concerning the requirements of the heavenly Kingdom *(Matt 5:-20).* However, conformity to Christ's own teachings pre-supposes that He is the Messiah; that He came to fulfill the Law and the Prophets and that what He teaches and declares is the morality of the Kingdom of God relating to the totality of life, inward and outward, seen by God. Our Lord made it clear that the norms of the teaching of the Scribes and Pharisees are an inferior to the righteous living that God required; He contrasts it with the proper righteousness He exhibits and proclaims and looks for *(Luke 5:30-32)* in the disciples of the Kingdom. Therefore, in a fundamental sense, in the four gospels, righteousness as the quality of living is intimately related to the arrival and membership in the Kingdom of God and is only possible because God has come to His people as their Redeemer. The gospel of Mathew declared that God from the beginning of Jesus' mission is to fulfill God's righteousness *(Matt 3:15).* This is brought to the realization in His words and in His earthly ministry, so that the Kingdom of God and salvation of God are in Him and come through Him. He came to the world to do the Father's will, which is the righteousness in the New Covenant, which is right thinking, right feeling, speaking, and right behavior on the part of all the disciples of the Kingdom, who do what God approves and commands. What our Lord Jesus Christ teaches and proclaims, outlines certainly not a self-righteousness for it is portrayed as the outflowing of a life that is centered on submitting to, worshiping, and seeking after God and confessing Christ as the Messiah *(Matt 5:7- 42).*

In the gospel of Luke, Zechariah, Elisabeth, Simon, and Joseph of Arimathea are being righteous because they embody genuine religion according to the Old Testament Covenant; they trust and obey God. Jesus Christ Himself, servant and Son of God is the righteous, innocent one, even as the Centurion confessed at the Cross. The righteousness of the Kingdom of God is practical and reverses the standards of the regular social order. On the Last Day, those who are genuinely righteous in terms of doing the will of God, will be declared just, as God is righteous *(17:15);* and the Holy Spirit, the Paraclete has a specific role with respect to the righteousness *(16:8, 10).* It is the unique work of the Holy Spirit who comes to the world in the name of Jesus Christ the Messiah, to indicate, convince, and convict the world of righteousness. The Spirit vindicates Jesus Christ as the Righteous One, whom the Father raised from the dead and exalted into heaven, and who also makes clear what kind of righteous life is required by and in grace, provided by God. God acts righteously when He performed saving deeds for His people and thereby, delivered them, and placed them in a right relationship with Himself *(Isaiah 51 & 61)*. The interchangeability of righteousness and salvation is clearly seen in the Holy Scripture*: "I am bringing my righteousness near, it is not far away, and my salvation will not be delayed. I will grant salvation to Zion, my splendor to Israel"* (Isaiah 46:13); God's people are righteous when they are in right relationship with Him when they enjoy His salvation; they are considered by God as the Judge of the world as righteous when they are being and doing what He requires in His covenant. God's righteousness is God's saving activity in and through the life, death and resurrection of Jesus Christ, His Son. The activity directly in line with God's saving plan from the Old Testament to the New Testament acceptance of the unique saving deed of God at Calvary by faith in Jesus Christ, which God has ordained to the means of saving the sinners and the lost, the unrighteous, and the disobedient people, so that they can enter into a right relationship with God the Father, and receive forgiveness, which is in Jesus Christ. God is the One wants all the believing Christians to become righteous indeed by faith, and love. Righteousness based on the fulfillment of the Law, it is righteousness by faith in Christ Jesus our Lord and Savior.

# SONG OF PRAISES

*My faith looks up to Thee,*

*Thou Lamb of Calvary,*

*Savior divine!*

*Now hear me while I pray,*

*Take all my guilt away,*

*O let me from this day*

*Be Wholly Dine.*

*May thy rich grace impart*

*Strength to my fainting heart,*

*My zeal inspire;*

*As thou as died for me,*

*O may my love to thee*

*Pure, warm, and changeless be,*

*A living fire.*

*While life's dark maze I tread,*

*And griefs around me spread;*

*Be thou my guide;*

*Bid darkness turn to day,*

*Wipe sorrows' tears away.*

*nor let me ever stray*

*From thee aside.*

*When ends life's transient dream,*

*When death's cold sullen stream*

*Shall o'er me roll,*

*Blest Savior, then in love*

*Fear and distrust remove;*

*O bear me safe above,*

*A ransomed soul.*

*(Hymn 580)*

# CHAPTER NINE

# THE MERCY OF GOD

The Mercy of God in Christ Jesus our Lord is a concentration to the understanding of God's presence with the people of this world that He created. God is a merciful and mighty God compassionate full of truth and righteousness. Merciful describes the quality of God and all that God is to His people. God Almighty is full of love and mercy to everyone in this Universe. God's loving-kindness and compassion, "pity" means to show mercy. The Holy Scripture says, *"It is of the Lord's mercies that we are not consumed, because his compassions failed not. They are new every morning; great is thy faithfulness,"* *(Lamentations 3:22-23 KJV).* From the Old Testament to the New Testament mercy is part of God's nature. Human beings have the capacity for showing mercy; especially toward those they have a personal relationship with, such as their friends and relatives. Lack of mercy is common to the human condition and it is natural mercy is, however, a quality intrinsic to the nature of God. It is for this reason that God in so many situations always exercises His mercy upon us. Mercy is one of the important expressions of God's nature; that children particularly observe and recount through experience God's mercy, which is different from human mercy. The Divine mercy of God is always alive and shines upon His people. Mercy is the foundation of God's covenant.  God's covenant love, are very integrally related to human troubles.

In God's relationship to His creation, mercy comes to be seen as the quality in God that directs and protects His people.  Mercy is also manifested in God's activities on behalf of His people to free them from the bondage of slavery of sin.  God's mercy is mediated through the covenant, by which He becomes the God of people promising, protecting, provision, guidance and constant presence *(Ps 23:6)* because God is the initiator; the mercy He gives is gracious, unmerited and undeserved *(Genesis 19:16)*. God's mercy brought forgiveness, a basic disposition to compassion and to the steadfast love by which God sustains the covenant, which results in repeated forgiveness of sin of His people in the Old Testament.  In the New Testament God's convenience of mercy continues; God desires a relationship with all the people on earth.  But God shows His mercy through Jesus Christ, which is the supreme expression of love, mercy, and through the grace of God.  Apostle Peter stated, "Once you were not a people, but now you are the people of God; once you had not received mercy, but now you have received mercy," *(1st Peter 2:10).* God's mercy is also displayed in the New Testament ministry of Jesus Christ, which again is the greatest of mercy that God has shown to everyone in the world.  Jesus Christ healed the sick, cleansed the Lepers, and woke up the dead.  Our Lord drove away demons from the man in the tomb and told him to go back to his home and tell his people how God showed mercy on him *(Mark 5:19).* God Almighty has mercy on the sick through Jesus Christ.  Mercy was manifested in practical help; God was merciful and sympathetic with their affliction.  God is the same yesterday, today, and forever.

Mercy is the foundation of salvation Jesus Christ demonstrated in individual lives the mercy of God pleases and releases us from sin and death. The fundamental factor in every activity of God is mercy. God's compassionate love for the people of this earth in salvation rests on God's mercy for humankind. By His great mercy, He has given us a new life through the resurrection of Jesus Christ from the dead. *"He saved us not because of any works of righteousness that we had done, but according to His mercy," (Ephesians 2:4-5).* God's mercy throughout in the New Testament display, shows clearly to the people of this world through Jesus Christ, His only Son. God's mercy and compassion activity on behalf of those who are around us are the essence of spiritual living and spiritual awakening. True Christian faith produces genuine mercy towards those in need. It is the characteristic of mercy that made Jesus Christ go among all kinds of people and help them during His earthly ministry. All the believing Christians in the world must show mercy to all the people around them, not only to Christians, but also to the sinners and the lost. With this show of mercy, they can be converted and be saved. Christian believers, let us display the mercy of God in all the areas of our lives.

# SONG OF PRAISES

*Praise to the Lord, the Almighty, the*

*King of creation*

*O my soul, praise him, for he is thy*

*Health and salvation:*

*Come, ye who hear,*

*Brothers and sisters, draw near,*

*Praise him in glad adoration.*

*Praise to the Lord, who o'er all things*

*So wondrously reigneth.*

*Shelters thee under his wings, yea, so*

*Gently sustaineth;*

*Hast thou not seen?*

*All that is needful hath been*

*Granted in what he ordaineth.*

*Praise to the Lord, who doth prosper*

*thy work and defend thee;*

*surely his goodness and mercy here*

*daily attend thee;*

*Ponder anew*

*All the Almighty can do,*

*He who with love doth befriend thee.*

*Praise to The Lord! O let all that is in*

*me adore him!*

*All that hath life and breath come now*

*with praises before him!*

*Let the Amen*

*Sound from His people again:*

*Gladly for ay we adore him!*

(Hymn626)

# CHAPTER TEN

## THE PEACE OF GOD IN JESUS CHRIST

The word peace means the opposite of violence, disturbances, hostilities, or freedom from internal and external strife in various ways. We totally rest on the love and mercy of God means to completely in Christ Jesus our Lord and Savior. Completely made whole by God. The Holy Scripture says, "Rest is for the people of God." The Hebrew name for peace is "shalom" as the wholeness of life. A means of right relationship between two parties, or between two nations. Example of the covenant of peace with the people of Israel by God which was always renewed or maintained. With a "Peace Offering" *(Ezekiel 34:25-26)*. Peace as a prosperity success, or the fulfillment *(Lev 26:3-9)* and Peace Shalom as the victory over the enemies, or as the sign of the absence of war. Please always use it as a greeting, as well as a farewell or goodbye. It is the fact of blessings, as we always greet each other in the church that "the peace of God be with each of us", as also when we say, *" May you be filled with good health, prosperity, victory, peace and the love of our God."* It is an expression of completeness and safety in the hands of our Lord. God Almighty is the channel and source of our peace. He alone is the source of peace for His name is Peace, "Yahweh Shalom" *(Judge 6:14)*. The Lord came down to the sinful human being, both Jew and the Gentile. He desired to enter into a covenant relationship with us. He established the covenant of Peace which was sealed with His presence; He established a perfect peace with all of His creations, as long as we maintain a high relationship with Him *(Isaiah 26:3)*. The God of peace mediated peace by sending His son to reconcile us to Him. Peace with God is the same through Jesus Christ's death and resurrection *(Rm 5:1)*. Apostle Peter said to Cornelius, *"You know the message of God sent to the people of Israel, telling the good news of peace through Jesus Christ, who is the Lord of all, the Savior of all,"* *(Acts 10:36)*. The Lord established a relationship of righteousness of peace, which resulted in the participation of abundance peace like a river, but peace may not work if people did not live their lives according to the will of God, and orders in righteousness. The God of peace and the peace of God will sanctify all the children of God *(1st Thessalonians 5:23)*. Apostle Paul made it clear, *"There will be trouble and distress for everyone who do evil."* First for the Jew and then for the Gentile; but glory, honor, and peace for everyone who does good. First for the Jew and then for the Gentile *(Rm 2:9-10)*. The Scripture says: *"The nations of the world will come under the dominion of the Prince of Peace so therefore, they will bear their sword into plowshares and their spears into pruning hooks(Isaiah 2:4) You shall go out with joy and be led forth in peace; The mountains and hills will burst into song before you and all the trees of the field will clap their hands"* *(Isaiah 55:12; 11:6-11)* Animals, the wolf and the Lamb and leopard will play with the children.

# SONG OF PRAISES

*Praise, my soul, the king of heaven;*

*To his feet thy tribute brings.*

*Ransomed, healed, restored, forgiven,*

*Who like me his praise should sing?*

*Praise him! Praise Him!*

*Praise the everlasting King.*

*Praise him for his grace and favor*

*To our father in distress;*

*Praise still the same for ever,*

*Slow to chide, and swift to bless.*

*Praise him! Praise him!*

*Glorious in his faithfulness.*

*Father-like, he tends and spares us;*

*Well our feeble frame he knows;*

*In his hands he gently bears us,*

*Rescues us from all our foes,*

*Praise him! Praise him*

*widely as his mercy flows*

*Angels, help us adore him:*

*Ye behold him face to face;*

*Sun and moon, bow down before him,*

*Dwellers all in time and space,*

*Praise him! Praise him!*

*Praise with us the God of grace.*

*(Hymn623)*

# CHAPTER ELEVEN

## PERSECUTION OF CHRISTIANS IN THE WORLD

Persecution for one's faith and righteousness of God has been going on from Old Testament to the New Testament and till this present age.  Prophet Jeremiah was persecuted and a prophet that was imprisoned *(Jeremiah 37 & 38).*

But God Almighty sent help to Jeremiah and he was rescued.  The Lord God sent prophet Jeremiah to the King Zedekiah to give him a message.  Jeremiah stood before the King confidently and unwaveringly proclaimed the word of the Lord.  He did not hesitate to announce the unpopular word that the city will be destroyed *(Jeremiah 37:8-10).*  He was beaten and imprisoned, under the threat of death, which did not cause him to waver from faithfulness to the Lord and to what God wanted him to deliver and say to them.  The official Army of Judah was very hostile to Prophet Jeremiah because of what he said to them.  They confined him to an underground dungeon.  He would have to die in the dark and dangerous cell had he remained there longer.  Jeremiah was put in a cistern;  he suffered greatly for  maintaining  his  faithfulness  to God and His message.  Up till today those who are faithful to God's revelation  and  righteousness  in  this  world  are  richly  persecuted because of unrighteousness in this world *(Matthew 5:10).*

God sent Ebed Melech, to Jeremiah; he rescued him by appealing to the King. Bed-Melech showed compassion to Jeremiah and courage in opposing the prophet's enemies. Christian believers must always try to help those who are being persecuted, mistreated for their faith, even if it means standing against the opposition. God spared Jeremiah's life; God also spared the life of Ebed-Melech, when Jerusalem fell; God did not forget His true servant who rescued Jeremiah. In the New Testament the Early Church were severely persecuted for their faith in Jesus Christ. Ready to be killed, and in response to the Church's praying, an angel of the Lord rescued Peter. Peter came, knocking at the door, and they didn't even know it was him. *"So Peter was kept in prison, but the church was earnestly praying to God for him. The night before Herod was to bring him to trial, Peter was sleeping between two soldiers, bound with two chains, and sentries stood guard at the entrance. Suddenly an angel of the Lord appeared and a light shone in the cell. He struck Peter on the side and woke him up. Quick, get up! he said, and the chains fell off Peter's wrists. But Peter kept on knocking, and when they opened the door and saw him, they were astonished,"* (Acts Chapter 12: 5-7;16 NIV).

Apostle Paul was imprisoned and martyred in Rome by Nero Claudius Caesar Augustus Germanicus who ruled the Roman Empire from 54-68 AD persecuting all the Christians. Caesar Augustus died June 9th, 68AD (Encyclopedia Britannica Quick Facts). Stephen was stoned to death and while he was dying, he saw the Lord standing in heaven to welcome Him. Peter was crucified upside down when he was martyred because he told them that, he was not worthy to be crucified the same way with his Lord and Savior *(Acts)*. Persecution comes in so many ways, such as harassment, oppression, and all kinds of evil punishment, such as (suicide bombers) *(Luke 17:23; Matthew 5:11-12).*

Affliction is one of the forms of persecution.  The Scripture revealed clearly the objects of the persecution teaches that those who follow Jesus Christ and God's Word and who practice the Ten Commandments will be persecuted.  Abel was persecuted by Cain for  offering a better  sacrifice than Cain *(Genesis 4:4-10).*  Elijah was persecuted because he defeated the prophet of Baal *(1st King 18:25-40)* and spoke against Idolatry of Israelites; he was persecuted by Jezebel who vowed to kill him *(1st King 19:1-3).*  In the New Testament, John the Baptist, who spoke out against the adultery of King Herod Antipas, was beheaded *(Mark 6:21-29).* Stephen, one of the elders in the Early Church, who preached the Gospel before the Sanhedrin and proclaiming God's Judgment because of sin of the people was stoned to death *(Acts 6:5-7 1-10).* Paul who was persecuted, beaten, and imprisoned as he preached from place to place, was killed in Rome *(2nd Timothy 4:6-8).*  Our Lord Jesus Christ Himself who preached God's grace and judgment *(Matthew 4:17;11:28-29)* was persecuted by His people.  He was rejected by His hearers; they plotted against Him, and He was crucified dead and buried then raised to life *(Luke 13:34).*  The reasons for persecution is because people of this world did not want to know the truth of God's Word.  The evil people persecuting the good people and righteous people, because they preached the Gospel and the condemnation of rebellion against God *(Acts 7:54-60)* because they stand for Jesus Christ.  Christians believers, servants were being insulted, deprived of clothing, clothed in sheep-skin and goats skin, destitute wandering in the desert and mountains in caves and holes in the ground were tortured, sawed in two, jailed, flogged, chained, shot, put to death by the mouth of lions, put to death by the sword *(Hebrews 11:36-38)*. The main reason for persecution is because people loved evil more than good.  They opposed God's love and His divine precepts *(Rm 13:10-18)*.  Our Lord indicated that as the world hated Him, they will also hate His disciples and His followers *(John 15:18-19)* and as they persecuted Him, they will also persecute all those who believed in Him. *"Everyone who wants to live a godly life in Christ will be persecuted,"* (2nd Timothy 3:12).  Our Lord said if they persecuted Me, they will persecute you also *(John 15:20)*.  Therefore, all the Christian believers, let us fix our eyes on Jesus, the author and perfecter of our faith *(Hebrews 12:2)*.

# SONG OF PRAISES

*Rock of Ages, cleft for me.*

*Let me hide myself in thee;*

*Let the water and the blood,*

*From thy riven side which flowed,*

*Be of sin the double cure:*

*Cleanse me from its guilt and power.*

*Not the Labor of my hands*

*Can fulfill thy law's demands*

*Could my zeal no respite know,*

*Could my tears for ever flow,*

*All for sin could not atone;*

*Thou mu save, and Thou alone.*

*Nothing in my hand I bring:*

*Simply to thy cross I cling;*

*naked, come to thee for dress;*

*Helpless look to Thee for grace;*

*Foul, I to the fountain fly:*

*Wash me, Savior, or I die.*

*While I draw this fleeting breath,*

*When mine eyes are closed in death,*

75

*When I soar though tracts unknown,*

*See thee on thy judgment throne:*

*Rock of ages, cleft for me,*

*Let  hide myself in thee.*

*(Hymn636)*

# CHAPTER TWELVE

## THE GREAT COMMISSION OF OUR LORD AND SAVIOR

The Great Commission is a mandatory assignment for all the believing Christians in the world the very moment you give your life to Jesus Christ.  He blessed you with his Holy Spirit and gave you the assignment of the Great Commission.  Our Lord said that as the Father sent me, so I have sent you, go and make the disciples of all the people in all the nations of the Earth. *(Matthew 28:16-20).* Because Jesus Christ has been given all authority in heaven and on the Earth, the Great Commission must be taken with the utmost seriousness by all the disciples and all the believing Christians to the very end of the age.  The Great Commission came from the heart of God.  God so loved the world, he gave us His Son *(John 3:16).* The disciples and all the Christian believers are sent out to the world to accomplish what God had started in sending His Son to the world *(John 20:21).* The Great Commission is linked to God's words to Abraham that *"all the people on earth will be blessed through him..." (Genesis 2:3).* The Great Commission is accomplished through the witnessing, preaching, baptizing, and teaching of the Gospel. *(Mark 28:20)* "Then Jesus came to them and said, *'All authority in heaven and on earth has been given to me. Therefore go and make disciples of all nations, baptizing them in the name of the Father and of the Son and of the Holy Spirit, and teaching them to obey everything I have commanded you.  And surely I am with  you always, to the very end of the age' " (Matthew 28: 16-20).*

Jesus' disciples are to replicate themselves in the lives of those who respond to the Good News of the Gospel.  The Holy Spirit is the empowering agent for those who witness *(Acts 1:8)*, as well as connecting the sinners of their need for salvation through Jesus Christ *(John 16:8-11*).  The disciples will have success because Jesus the Lord of heaven and Earth will be with them as they undertake their assignments.  The Great Commission necessitates the Gospel message to the end of the Earth. *(Acts 1:8)*  To all nations, the Good News is to be shared with all the peoples for all are sinners, both Jew and the Gentiles, and in need of Savior to deliver them from the bondage and slavery of sin.  All the people in the world by faith can receive God's provision and are baptized into Jesus Christ.  In Jesus Christ, all the distinctions between Jew and the Gentiles disappear. *(Romans 10:12-13)*

# SONG OF PRAISES

*Christ, whose glory fills the skies,*

*Christ, the true, the only Light,*

*Sun of righteousness, arise,*

*Triumph o'er the shades of night;*

*Dayspring from on high, be near;*

*Dark and cheerless is the morn*

*Unaccompanied by thee;*

*Joyless is the day's return,*

*Till thy mercy's beams I see;*

*Till they inward light impart,*

*Glad my eyes, and warm my heart.*

*Visit then this soul of mine;*

*Pierce the gloom of sin and grief;*

*Fill me, radiance divine,*

*Scatter all my unbelief;*

*More and more thyself display,*

*Shining to the perfect day. (Hymn26)*

*(13)*

*Forth in thy name, O Lord, I go,*

*My daily labor to pursue;*

*Thee, only Thee, resolved to know,*

*In all, I think, or speak, or do.*

*Preserve me from my calling's snare,*

*And hide my simple heart above;*

*Above the thorns of choking care,*

*The gilded baits of worldly love,*

*Thee may I set at my right hand,*

*Whose eyes my most substance see.*

*And labor on at thy command,*

*And offer all my works to thee.*

*Give me to bear thy easy yoke,*

*And every moment watch and pray,*

*And still to things eternal look.*

*And hasten to thy glorious day:*

*For thee delightfully employ*

*Whate'er thy bounteous grace hath*

*Given,*

*And run my course with even joy,*

*And closely walk with thee to heaven.*

*(Hymn29)*

# CHAPTER THIRTEEN

# PRAYER STUDY FROM THE OLD TESTAMENT
# TO THE NEW TESTAMENT

Prayer from the Old Testament to the New Testament reveals beliefs, or assumptions, that underline the practice of all the Christians. Our Lord Jesus Christ gave us the model of prayer life.

Prayer is a petition which includes:

Adoration Psalms 144-150 in the Old Testament;

The book of Luke, chapter 1:46-55, Confession of Sins: Psalm 51; Luke 18:13-14; &

Thanksgiving Prayers: Psalm 75; 1st Thessalonian 1:2.

Christian prayers have always been Petitionary. Elijah prays that there should be no rain for three years and there was no rain. He prayed again and the rain comes.

Jesus Christ, our Lord prayed that Lazarus would come out of the grave, raised from the dead after 4 days.

Elijah's triumph over the Priest of Baal *(1st King 8:22-65; 17; 18:20-46).*

The Lord answered Elijah's petition.

The Christians' beliefs from Old Testament to the New Testament that clearly revealed that God could be petitioned, called:

To intervene and bring effective changes in the lives of individuals, nature, and in all the worldly events.

Our Lord Jesus Christ taught us how to petition daily to God. He taught us to pray the "The Lord's Prayer" in the book of *Matthew 6:9-13; Luke 1:2-4.* He wants us to ask the Father for all of our daily needs *(Matthew 7:7; Luke 1:9).* Our petition is to let God know the desire of our hearts and the assurance that He is the only one that can fulfill the desire of our hearts, as He knows what is good for us. Prayer petition is between the divine and human - the fundamental belief that we are communicating with our heavenly Father, whom we cannot see, but He is always actively present when we kneel down to pray. God Who listened and answered prayers in the Old Testament to the New Testament *(Genesis 21:16-18; 22:11-12),* reveal also: God's intentions, human beings questions, requests and requests for guidance, to include our complaints, and reasons for complaints in the book of Genesis.

In chapters 15, 18, 21, 22, 28 of the Exodus chapters, to include: 3, 5, 32; all these Old Testament Scriptures maintained and strengthened our personal relationship with God in our prayers. We fellowship and communicate with the Father, Son, and the Holy Spirit in the New Testament - called Him Master, servant, child, Father, and Bridegroom . From the Old Testament to the New Testament where Christ taught us the Fatherhood of God, to include that He is the same God from the Old Testament to the New Testament. God is our heavenly Father, that we communicate with him intimately and sincerely as a child communicates with an earthly father: *Mark chapter 14, Matthew*

*11, Luke 11.* Our Lord wants everyone on Earth to communicate, pray to the Father in the same way Christ prayed to the Father. God Almighty is the supreme being of the Universe, the Omnipresent, omnipotent, and Omniscient. He can do more than we ask from Him. He is a sovereign God over us and He has perfect control over the Earth. He is the source of and bestowed all good things; He opens His hands, and we receive every good thing. When He closes His hands, we lack. He is the God of all provisions. Human beings receive both spiritual and physical gifts from God. Prayer must also result, and be offered in perfect obedience: *1st Samuel chapter 7, and 15* - Samuel's intercession for King Saul in the Old Testament.

Prayer produces encouragement, guidance, and power of the Holy Spirit *(the book of Acts: 8, 10, 13, 16, 18, 23; James chapter 5.)*

The true basis of prayer is when there is a remembering of what God has done in the past: He will strengthen and guide the petitioner to make his or her request be known more and more.

In the book of Deuteronomy (chapters 4,9,32) which also shows and reveals the remembrance of God's loving-kindness: *Genesis chapter 32; 1st King chapter 3*).

Then there is also God's covenantal relationship with the children of Israel, such as salvation history *(Matthew 6; 2nd King chapter 19).*

# CHAPTER FOURTEEN

## PRAYING IN THE NAME OF JESUS CHRIST

Prayer is a response to God's activities, and a divine act of God's revelation in Jesus Christ, whom all the promises of God are fulfilled.  All believing Christians pray with the indwelling of the Holy Spirit that indwells and abides in us as noted below:

The role of our Lord Jesus Christ and the Holy Spirit, as Christians must pray in Jesus Christ name *(John chapter 14, 16)*.

It signifies that the prayer petitioner takes the attitude of Christ Jesus toward God and toward the Universe.  To pray in Jesus Christ's name means that praying is to pray in a manner that consists with our Identification.  This is affected by the reconciliation of God and humans.  Praying in Jesus Christ's name means that Jesus Christ is like a password that that can be used without discrimination by every human being in the world.

Praying in Jesus name is an identification of a person who prays with the right methods or conditions of prayer the book of Acts, chapter 19.  It is a prayer that protects Christians from misreading of God's nature and His Will; it saves petitioner from human selfishness.  It is a prayer that keeps with God's Will, which also reveals in our Lord's Prayer that says; "God's Will be done on earth has it is written in heaven." Expressed by the divine economy in Jesus Christ, God's Will be done through us and in us.  We may be an obedient servant and a child of God in our accomplishments.

Christian prayer is mediated by Jesus Christ, where the role of Jesus Christ began, when He ascended to heaven to the Father and seated at His right hand.  Where He empathizes with our condition and been our heavenly Mediator in prayer asking the Father for what we needed.

Christ Jesus our ultimate intercessor, Christian prayer becomes intercession; it is presented through and by Christ to God the Father because without the intercession of Jesus Christ; we cut ourselves off from the benefits of our petition.  Jesus Christ is the only hope, our hope of glory that our prayer will be heard by His mediatorial role.  Seal your prayer with His full Great Holy Name; a Name Above all names in Heaven and on Earth.

# CHAPTER FIFTEEN

## THE HOLY SPIRIT GUIDED PRAYER BY PRAYING IN THE SPIRIT

Jesus Christ is the Mediator of a New Covenant. Christian prayer is prompted and guided by the Holy Spirit. The Holy Spirit helps us to pray to God as our Father "Abba" *(Romans chapter 8; Galatians, Chapter 4)*. The Holy Spirit's role is variously interpreted; it is usually associated with the regulations, purification of our hearts' request as the interpreter of the mind of God. The Holy Spirit is the controller; director, and interpreter of our hearts desire – *(2nd Corinthian chapters 12)*.

In prayer we wrestle with God, we sometime struggle with God in our prayers. The book of Psalms and at Peniel where Jacob wrestled with God gave us examples of wrestling in prayer to God.

Another example of wrestling in prayer is Jacob in *Genesis, Chapter 32*. Jacob engaged and wrestled with God with perseverance that refuses to let God go until Jacob's desire was fulfilled. Jacob's wrestle with God changes his character, and put a mark on him for life, and his name was changed to Israel. Jacob wrestled with God till daybreak. Then the man ask him what is your name? Jacob answered, my name is Jacob The man said your name will no longer be Jacob, Israel, because you have struggled with God and with men and have overcome. The book of *Genesis 32:22-32* is our prayer is to overcome any troubles and afflictions.

Other examples in the Old Testament is in *Jeremiah, Chapter 12).*

*Habakkuk, Chapter 1* which shows clearly the results and assurances that all is in God's control and as well deepened the understanding of God's purposes and providence.

In the New Testament, Jesus Christ at the Garden of Gethsemane prayer *(Matthew, Chapter 26).* We also see Paul's Thorn- in -the-flesh prayer *(2nd Corinthians, Chapter 2:1-24).*

Our Lord teaches us importunity in Prayer *(Luke chapter 5-13)*; this parable teaches perseverance, continuing in praying and asking, knocking on the door, and seeking in our requests and heart's desires until our circumstances change.

# WORDS OF KNOWLEDGE: FRUIT OF THE HOLY SPIRIT

Prayer is a time that we repent of our sins and confess it to the Lord. At the prayer, we demand of God-ordained blessings for our life needs, and attacks of the enemies for our life. Prayer is a time that God releases His benefits and blessings for our life. Divine promises and the supernatural power supplies of God opens our demands on God-ordained benefits, and all of our needs and wants is open to Hm in the place of prayer. Prayer gives us the power, focusing on our inheritance in God and the faith in the Almighty. This is the reason why we need our daily devotional prayer; that helps to open our hearts and minds to God and approach Him has a child demands what he or she needs from our heavenly Father.

At the time of prayer, is when God gives us what we ask of Him in Scripture: *James: "Ye have not, because you ask not," (James 4:2).* Prayer is our counsel, and it is when our mind and hearts' access Divine promises and supernatural supplies.  Our demands on God-ordained benefits, and attach needs and wants in our life at the place of prayer. Prayer is an alter where we attack the enemy for our needs and wants in our lives, as well as everything that is necessary for life and Godliness. Scripture says, *"His divine power has given us everything we need for life and godliness through our knowledge of him who called us by His own glory and goodness." (2nd Peter 1:3).*

Scripture: *"Give us this day our daily bread," (Matthew 6:11-15).*  At the time and at the place of prayer, we demand the benefits that God-ordained for our lives.  Prayer is where we make demands on God's supernatural supplies that are abundantly beyond natural.

Prayer is a platform we receive by faith and the delivery of divine packages; we receive the delivery of what has been packaged for us at the place of prayer by God. Prayer is the platform for accessing divine promises of God.  Prayer gives us the platform to accessing our inheritance in God through Jesus Christ our Lord and Savior.  This is what our Jesus Christ means when He taught us how to pray.

Regardless, of how tall you are, you cannot see tomorrow. Use the fruit of the Holy Spirit – Patience. When you die; regardless of how big and strong you are, you cannot carry yourself to your grave. Use the fruit of the Holy Spirit – humbleness.  Regardless of your skin color black, white, brown, pink, and light skinned, you still need light in darkness; be careful, be warned – love. You still need the love of God which is in Christ Jesus Our Lord. The Scripture revealed: *"If I speak in the tongues of men and angels, but have no love, I am only a resounding gong or a clanging cymbal... Love is patient, love is kind, it does not envy, it does not boast is not proud..." (1st Corinthians 13:1-4).* Even rich billionaires, or the richest man on Earth, and even the poorest man on Earth, and even if one owned many gold cars, or silver cars, and many cars, you still have to always walk to your bed when you are ready to sleep.  Use the fruit of the Holy Spirit, gentleness.  All the Christian believers must know what life they live!!!  No one live is on this Earth forever.

# CHAPTER SIXTEEN

# HOW GOD ANSWERS OUR PRAYER OR OUR PETITION

Christ teaches us how God answers our petitions in prayer. The wrestling in prayer can change God's Will or the circumstances, and God's response to prayer. God always listens to our prayers and answers our prayers, according to our petition as noted below:

(1) If what we ask for what is good for us;

(2) God answers prayer but it is not yet time - wait for the appointed time.

(3) God answers prayer if it is according to His Will. God answer prayers: *Psalm 3, 6, 17, 138; Matthew, Chapter 7).*

Sometimes God could be silent to our prayers; this means He is doing something in our lives more than what we asked from Him: *(Psalms 10, 13, 77, 89).*

Our sins might not let God hear, or answer our prayers. We have to pray for the forgiveness of our known and unknown sins: *(Psalms 51, Deuteronomy 3, psalm 66, Isaiah 1; 59 James chapters*

(4) God can also give us examples, as in the life of Job. Pray according to the Will of God, as well as prayer that is prayed and expressed in Jesus Christ.

God's silence to prayer is temporary and will never be permanent: *(Psalm 22 and 28).*  There are some prayers that are answered in a way that we do not expect, because we did not hear the response; we want to hear does not mean that the Lord did not answer our prayers

Often,  He has something better for us.  Prayer might not be answered because we do not pray in Jesus Christ's Name or according to God's Will for us, or for the entire Universe.  God graciously, faithfully, and mercifully answers prayers according to His divine promises for us and for everyone on Earth.

God Almighty exercises and exhibits His power from the Old Testament to the New Testament :  We need to read the book of *Habakkuk, Chapters 3,5-6, 9-16* and *Psalms 68:20-23.*

*"One day the angels came to present themselves before the Lord; and Satan answered also came with them. The Lord said to Satan, 'Where have you come from?' Satan answered the Lord, "From roaming through the earth and going back and forth in it," Then the Lord said to Satan, 'Have you considered my servant Job?...(Job Chapter 1:6-8a)' "* Job was blameless meaning he was a mature worshiper of God whose conscience was clear.  He was a man of integrity, wholesome in his attitudes and righteous in his lifestyles.

*Another Scripture revealed: Jacob wrestles with God, " That night Jacob got up and took his two wives, his two maidservants and his eleven sons and crossed the ford of the Jacob.  After he had sent them across the stream, he sent over all his possessions. So Jacob was left alone, and a man wrestled with him, till daybreak. When the man saw that he could not overpower him, he touched the socket of Jacob's hip, so that his hip was wrenched as he wrestled with the man. Then the man said, 'Let me go, for it is daybreak.' But Jacob replied, 'I will not let you go unless you bless me,' The man asked him. 'What is your name?' Jacob, he answered. Then the man said, 'Your name will no longer be Jacob, but Israel, because you have struggled with God and with men and have overcome,'" (Genesis Chapter 32:22-28).* His name changed to Israel which means he struggled with God; all the believers of Jesus Christ are sometimes called the "Israel of God" *(Galatians 6:16).*

# CHAPTER SEVENTEEN

# JESUS EXHIBITS HIS POWER OVER HUMAN AND NATURE

Power over the Storm: The power that God used over the sea during the Israelites' journey from Egypt is the same power He used to part the Red Sea and the Jordan River.

He told Moses say that I am sending you; this is the same power God used to create the world. *(Mark 4:40-41, 6:51-52; 47-50 4:39).* This is the same power Jesus Christ used to calm the storm and walk on the ocean. He told Nicodemus, *"You have to be born again of Water and the Spirit."* *(John, Chapter 3:1-21) (Psalm 107:28-30; Matthew chapter 14:22-33) (Mark 4:35-42 Mathew 8, 18: 23-27 Luke 8: 22-25)*

Leviticus *19:18* you shall not take vengeance, or bear any grudge against your neighbor.

The Lord God passed before Moses in the cloud and stood with him there, and proclaimed the Name of the Lord. God's love abides unto a thousand generations. *(Exodus chapter 57).*

God's covenant about discrimination: *(Amos 9:7-8).*

Parable of the Seed: The Seed is the Word of God: *(Luke 8:4-11, Isaiah 40:9-11 Jeremiah 23:2-3).*

Our Lord Jesus Christ Exhibit His power over by His power of healing the individual that call on Him during His earthly ministry and till today. The Scripture revealed: a man suffering with Leprosy in the *book of Matthew chapter 8:1-4, Mark Chapter1: 40-44;* He healed Peter's mother-in-law *(Matthew chapter 8:14-15)*; Christ exercised His power by healing the Roman Centurion's servant *(Luke chapter 7:1-10).* What about the two demon possessed men from Gadara in the *book of Mark Chapter 5:1-15;* The paralytic paralyzed man in the *book of Luke Chapter 5:18-26.* We must not forget about the woman with a twelve year bleeding issue *(Matthew Chapter 9:20-22).* Two blind men and healing of blind Bartimaeus, the son of Timaeus in the gospel of *Mark chapter 10:46-52, Luke chapter 18:35-43.* We must remember the Canaanite woman's daughter in the *book of Matthew chapter 15:21-28.*

Jesus Christ's exhibit His power on a sick who have been there for thirty-eight years at the Pool of Bethesda in the *book of John Chapter 5:1-15.* We must remember the man born blind Jesus healed his eyes in the *book of John chapter 9:1-41.* Jesus Christ exhibits His power on the ten men with leprosy that were healed and only one came back to give thanks in the *book of Luke chapter 17:11-19.* Healing of the sick in Gennesaret when they had crossed over, they came to land at Gennesaret and moored the boat. When they got out of the boat, people at once recognized Him, and rushed about that whole region and began to bring the sick on mats to wherever they heard He was and wherever He went, into villages, or cities or farms. They laid the sick in the marketplaces, and begged him that they might touch even the fringe of His cloak;

and all who touched it were healed revealed in the Scripture the *book of Mark chapter 6:53.*

Our Lord Jesus Christ has the power, and He exhibited His power and nature during His earthly ministry, calming down the raging storm. The Scripture revealed in the *book of Matthew chapter 8:23-27.* Our Lord's  feeding of  the five thousand people, not including children and women with five-loaves of bread and two fishes in the *book of Matthew chapter 14:1-21.*  Also feeding of the four thousand with seven loaves of bread and a few small fishes in the *book of Matthew chapter 15:32-39.* Christ exhibited His power over nature when He walked on the water in the *book of Matthew chapter 14:22-32.* Christ turned water into wine in the *book of John chapter 2:1-11.* Raising Jairus's  daughter in *Luke chapter 8:40-56.*  We must not forget the son of the widow at Nain's son the *book of Luke chapter 7:11-17.* Also, the waking up of Lazarus from the dead after four days in the tomb in the *book of John chapter 11:1-44.*

# CHAPTER EIGHTEEN

# IMPORTANT INFORMATION OF PRAYING IN JESUS CHRIST'S HOLY NAME

**Praying in Jesus Christ's name involves many valuable things:**

(1) Praying in harmony with his nature, character and according to his Will.

(2) Praying in Jesus Christ's name with faith in him and in his authority, and with the desire to glorify both the Father and the Son.

(3) Praying in the name of Jesus Christ, therefore, means that Jesus Christ will answer every prayer that he would have prayed himself.  There is no limit to the power of prayer when believers address their prayer to Jesus Christ, or to the Father in Holy Faith according to Jesus Christ's Desire and his Word and his Will; according to the direction of the power Holy Spirit.

*(4)* He said in the Holy Scripture:  *"Whatsoever you shall ask the Father in my name He will give it to you" (John 16:23).* Only those who have received the Lord Jesus Christ as their Lord and Savior can pray to God as Father.  We must always pray in Jesus Holy Name, if we want God the Father to

hear our prayer and answer our prayers. All the believing Christians must come to the Father through Jesus Christ our great intercessor in heaven. *"Therefore, since we have a great high Priest who has gone through the heavens, Jesus the Son of God, let us hold firmly to the faith we profess. For we do not have a high Priest who is unable to sympathize with our weaknesses, tempted in every way, just as we are – yet was without sin. Let us then approach the throne of grace with confidence; so that we may receive mercy and find grace to help us in our time of need,"* (Hebrews4:14-16).

It signifies that the prayer petitioner take the attitude of Christ Jesus toward God and toward the Universe.

To pray in Jesus Christ's name means that praying is to pray in a manner that consists with our Identification

This is affected by the reconciliation of God and human. Praying in Jesus Christ's name means that Jesus Christ

Is like a password that that can be used without discrimination by every human being in the world.

Praying in Jesus name is an identification of a person who prays with the right methods or conditions of prayer the Book of Acts chapter 19

It is a prayer that protects Christians from misreading of God's nature and his Will; it saves petitioner from human selfishness;

It is a prayer that keeps with God's Will, which also reveals in our Lord's Prayer that says; *"God's Will be done on earth has it is written in heaven;"*

Expressed by the divine economy in Jesus Christ.  God's Will be done through us and in us.  We may be an obedient servant and a child of God in our accomplishments.

Christian prayer is mediated by Jesus Christ, where the role of Jesus Christ began when he ascended to heaven to the Father and seated at His right hand.

Where He empathizes with our condition and been our heavenly mediator in prayer asking the Father for what we needed.

Christ Jesus our ultimate Intercessor, Christian prayer becomes intercession; it is presented through and by Christ to God the Father.

Because without the intercession of Jesus Christ; we cut ourselves off from the benefits of our petition.

Jesus Christ is the only hope, our hope of glory that our prayer will be heard by his mediatorial role.

Jesus Christ is the Mediator of a New Covenant.  Christian prayer is prompted and guided by the Holy Spirit.

The Holy Spirit helps us to pray to God has our Father "Abba" *Romans chapter 8; Galatian chapter 4.*

Holy Spirit's role is variously interpreted; it is usually associated with the regulations, purification of our heart's request as the interpreter of the mind of God.

Holy Spirit is the controller, director and interpreter of our hearts' desire - *2nd Corinthians chapter 12.*

In prayer we wrestle with God.  We struggle with God in our prayer.  The book of psalms and at Peniel where Jacob wrestle with God gave us examples of wrestling in prayer to God

Another example of wrestling in prayer is Jacob Genesis chapter 32.  Jacob engaged wrestled with God with perseverance that refuses to let God goes until Jacob's desire was fulfilled.  Jacob's wrestle with God change his character, and put a mark on him for life, his name was changed to Israel.   Other examples in the Old Testament is *Jeremiah chapter 12.*

Habakkuk chapter 1 which shows clearly the results and assurances that all is in God's control and as well deepened the understanding of God's purposes and Providence.

In the New Testament, Jesus Christ at the Garden of Gethsemane's prayer *Matthew chapter 26:14.*  We also see Paul's Thorn- in -the-flesh prayer (*2nd Corinthians Chapter 2:1-17).*

Our Lord Teaches us importunity in prayer *Luke chapter 11; 18*; parables teaches perseverance in our request until our request, hearts' desires, or our circumstances for our lives change.

Christ teaches us how God answer our petitions in prayer.  The wrestling in prayer can change God's Will or the circumstances and God's response to prayer.

 God always listen to our prayers and answers our prayers according to our petition: (1) if what we ask for is good for us; (2) God answers prayer but not yet time - wait for the appointed time.

(3) God answers prayer if it is according to His Will. God answer prayers: *Psalms 3, 6, 17, 138; Matthew chapter 7.*

Sometimes God could be silent to our prayers; this means He is doing something in our lives that is more than what we asked from Him: *Psalms 10, 13, 77, 89.*

Our sins might not let God hear, or answer our prayers; we have to pray for the forgiveness of our known and unknown sins: *(Psalms 51, Deuteronomy 3, psalm 66, Isaiah 1; 59 James, chapter 4).*

God can be licensed, example of Job.  Pray according to the Will of God, as well as prayer prayed and expressed in Jesus Christ.

God's silence to prayer is temporary and will never be permanent: *Example Psalm 22 and 28.*

There are some prayers that are answered in a way that we do not expect, because we did not hear the response; not receiving a response or want we want to hear, does not mean that the Lord did not answer our prayers.  He has something better for us.  Prayer might not be answered because we do not pray in Jesus Christ's Name, or according to God's Will for us, even for the entire Universe. God graciously, faithfully, and also mercifully answers prayers according to His Divine promises for us, and for everyone on Earth.

God Almighty exercises and exhibits His power from Old Testament to the New Testament :  We need to read the *Book of Habakkuk chapters 3,5-6, 9-16 Psalms 68:20-23.*

Power over the Storm: The power that God used over the sea during the Israelites journey from Egypt; the same power he used to part the Red Sea and the Jordan River.

He told Moses to say that "I AM" sent you; this is the same power God used when He created the world. (*Mark 4:40-41, 6:51-52; 47-50 4:39*).

*Leviticus 19:18* you shall not take vengeance, or bear any grudge against your neighbor.

The Lord God passed before Moses in the cloud and stood with him there, and proclaims the name of the Lord.  God's love abides unto a thousand generations (*Exodus chapter 57*).

God's covenant about discrimination: *Amos 9:7-8*

Parable of the Seed: The Seed is the Word of God:  *Luke 8:4-11, Isaiah 40:9-11 Jeremiah 23:2-3.*

The same Power Jesus Christ used to calm the Storm and walk on the Ocean. He told Nicodemus *"You have to be born again of Water and the Spirit,"* *(John chapter 3:1-21).*

*Psalm 107:28-30, Matthew chapter 14:22-33*

*Mark 4:35-42 Mathew 8, 18: 23-27 Luke 8: 22-25*

# CHAPTER NINETEEN

## CREATION

Man was created as the king of God's creation; we were created to be rulers on planet Earth.  And God said, *"Let us make man in our image, after our likeness: and let them have dominion over the fish of the sea, and over the fowl of the air, and over the cattle, and over all the earth, and over every creeping thing that crept upon the earth."* *(Genesis 1:26)*

As far as God is concerned, dominion over the entire creation is the destiny of man.  The creative mandate of God for man is dominion.  There is a creative agenda of God for us to reign as kings on the Earth.  This is confirmed in the account of creation in (Genesis 1:26-28).

So, man was created as the king of God's creation; we were created to be rulers on planet Earth.  It is true that man fell into sin, but God did not change his mind concerning His creative agenda for man.  That was why He went ahead to sacrifice His Son, Jesus, for our redemption.  This He did in order to cause His initial plan for man to stand for as many as would receive His Son Jesus Christ as their Lord and Savior.

The Devil may have attempted to corrupt our destiny, but God has not changed His mind about His people.  People may have given up on themselves, but God has not given up on them. We are still a chosen, royal, and peculiar people according to *1st Peter 2:9.* So, let it sink into our mind that from creation, and by redemption, God created us to reign and to be in charge.

There are three dimensions of dominion and authority that God has positioned us to exercise. We shall have two in this book and the third one in another book.

(1)      Dominion over Spiritual and Supernatural Forces

We are to exercise dominion over spiritual and supernatural forces *(Luke 10:19).* Beloved, you were created to dominate, control, and subdue principalities and powers, witches and wizards, demons, and devils. You were not created in the Image of God to be molested by a demon. You are in charge over satanic altars in your community and you must take your place in authority and dominion. Take charge!

Remember this: As far as God is concerned, dominion over the entire creation is the destiny of man.

During our Lord Jesus Christ's earthly ministry Scripture revealed:

*"'There is a lad here who has five barley loaves and two small fish, but what are they among so many?'" .Jesus took the loaves, and when He had given thanks He distributed them to the disciples, and the disciples to those sitting down; and likewise of the fish, as much as they wanted. So when they were filled...." (John 6:9-12 NKJV).*

*Galatians 4:7 says, "Wherefore thou art no more a servant, but a son; and if a son, then an heir of God through Christ." "For ye have not received the spirit of bondage again to fear; but ye have*

*received the Spirit of adoption, whereby we cry, Abba, Father."*
*(Romans 8:15)*

These Bible verses confirm that Christians are children of God who have received the birthright of sonship by grace, not merit. The grace of Abba Father will always work in our favor with the power of Jesus Christ and the ministry of the Holy Spirit.

The first privilege we enjoy as children of God is that we move from the position of servants to that of children and heirs. Thus, we must have a passion for evangelism especially for those who believe they are self-made slaves of sin after the fall of Adam. God did not create His image-carrier - man, for the purpose of making a slave out of him.

*Galatians 4:6-7 says, "And because ye are sons, God hath sent forth the Spirit of his Son into your hearts, crying, Abba, Father. Wherefore thou art no more a servant, but a son; and if a son, then an heir of God through Christ."*

In the story of the Syrophoenician woman in our text of today, Jesus Christ likened her to a dog, and she did not refute it. This is because the verdict was from the Way, the Truth, and the Life, He speaks with valid spiritual authority.

Liberal theologians who want to be 21st Century compliant would want to re-write the Bible to make it "politically correct." Some things, while politically correct, can be spiritually bankrupt.

To be fully become a child and part of the family of God, you need to be born again by faith in Jesus Christ. Let Him rinse you off and cleanse you in His precious blood *(Galatians 3:26).* The food of salvation, deliverance, healing, and prosperity meant for children of God will now become yours with the power of the Holy Spirit. If you are a born again Christian already, spread the Good News!

God's enduring and permanent glory shall remain immortalized in life of all the Christian believers in the world.

Scripture Reading: Genesis 12 vs. 1-3, Exodus 33 vs. 12-19, I Tim. 1 vs. 12-15.

Our Lord and Savior said, *"He that abided in me, and I in him, the same bring forth much fruit: for without me ye can do nothing,"* (John 15:5). Revival comes through total obedience to the Word of God. This is why the Bible admonishes us to preach the Word and spread the Good News of our Lord Jesus Christ as a matter of urgency.

However, Christians should wait to be sent forth and must never go alone, that is, without the Holy Spirit, says: *"And, behold, I send the promise of my Father upon you: but tarry ye in the city of Jerusalem, until ye be endued with power from on high."* (Luke 24:49)

Scripture revealed: *"So then faith cometh by hearing, and hearing by the word of God".* (Romans 10:17) At the hearing of the Word of God, the corrupt and sinful mind immediately begins to do a self-analysis, followed by personal conviction and repentance. *Romans 10:14 says, "How then shall they call on him in whom they have not believed? And how shall they believe in him of whom they have not heard? And how shall they hear without a preacher?"* However, all these will not yield the desired results unless the work is accompanied by the power of the Holy Spirit.

Scripture revealed: *"But ye shall receive power, after that the Holy Ghost is come upon you: and ye shall be witnesses unto me both in Jerusalem, and in all Judaea, and in Samaria, and unto the uttermost part of the earth."* (Acts 1:8)

As we strive to populate the Church building, we must remember our greater duty to prepare the people of God for heaven through the correct and unbiased teaching of the Word of God.

As you make up your mind to live in obedience to His Word, and take every opportunity to share the Gospel with at least one person daily, do not go without the Holy Spirit.  Every Christian needs the help of the Holy Spirit to fulfil the will of God for his/her life.  As you earnestly seek to be filled with the Holy Spirit, your prayers will be answered.

# CHAPTER TWENTY

## BUILDING RELATIONSHIP

The type of decision one takes in building a relationship or joining an association or taking any step in the journey of life would always affect one's life, progress, and destiny.

When you enter into a wrong or faulty partnership in any business endeavor? The end result is always failure and regrets and may even lead to untimely death.

When you refuse to involve God in the choice of your marriage partner, such a union will ultimately collapse, irreconcilably sooner or later.

When you decide to choose a wrong location of abode, it will eventually lead to discomfort, failure or one form of disappointment or the other.

You must bear in mind, that not everything that glitters is gold. Learn to prayerfully look beyond the ordinary and immediate benefits in choosing any acquaintances- in marriage or business relationship, and even in co-habitation with people, you are not conversant with their motives in planning a relationship with you.

Abraham chose to journey with Lot without consulting with God, but he later regretted his emotional actions. Jonah made a wrong move to relocate to a place not approved by God, it led to a great disaster that seriously affected his innocent co-travelers who lost everything except their lives.

God is always called a specialist in handling situations tagged impossible. He can use your case to demonstrate to the world that there is no situation, no matter how bad that He cannot reverse. Have you been waiting a long time for that precious promise of God to come to pass? Your season of divine visitation will come with the mighty power of God the Father, Son, and indwelling Holy Spirit.

Sarah-Abraham's wife, laughed at the prophecy of her having a baby within a year. She knew her age and the deadness of her husband's fertility system. Indeed, God had to ask: "Is anything too hard for the Lord? " *(Genesis 18:14)*

Christian believers who are overwhelmed by the doctor's report concerning their health, the report of the Lord will override every negative report.

Lazarus was dead and buried; his grave must have started to stink, yet the Lord moved into that hopeless situation and reversed the irreversible *(John 11:1-45)*.

Are you struggling with poverty? Have you been labelled a permanent failure? Have you been told that at your age, there is no miracle that can cause you to receive your heart's desire? If God sees that your season is naturally over, He reminds the world that He changes times and seasons *(Daniel 2:21)*. If the world boasts that they have finished your case, He reminds them that He knows what is in the darkness *(Daniel 2:22)*. I pray for an expedited reversal of every negative circumstance in your life today.

The Christian life is no ordinary natural existence; it is supernatural. It takes supernatural power to reverse the irreversible and move the immovable.

Believers will encounter the supernatural power of God, to the point where whatever was irreversible will be reversed, and whatever was immovable will be moved in the children of God's life.

God the Creator of heaven and Earth will shake the Earth and make the impossible possible in the nations and in this world.

The first responsibility of young believers after becoming born again is to desire the sincere milk of the Word, so that they may grow to maturity (1st Peter 2:2)

The anointing makes the difference between two weapons of warfare: The anointed one and the ordinary. David confirmed this in Psalm 20:7-8:

*"Some trust in chariots, and some in horses: but we will remember the name of the Lord our God. They are brought down and fallen: but we are raised, and stand upright."*

Beloved, regardless of how feeble your instrument of office or weapon of warfare may appear, you will do great development with it; provided you identify with the Anointed of the Almighty – Jesus Christ. Accept, follow, and obey His commandments today, and you will be victorious in all you do in life.

Vision is so vital for development in life and usually has its origin in the spiritual realm. Anyone with access to vision at any level is endowed with power to do great. That is why the bigger and clearer your vision, the greater your development.

It is important, by the help of the Holy Spirit, to be able to discern the times of your favor, or else you may miss them completely.  God is the revealer of secrets: *"For as many as are led by the Spirit of God, they are the sons of God." (Romans 8:14)*

The Holy Spirit could decide to use any available means to communicate with you – revealing deep secrets and telling you of things to come. It could be through a dream, revelation, vision, or an audible voice.  He could speak through a man of God at a program event, or He could send one to you directly.  Apostle Peter fished all night without a single catch, but because he was sensitive enough spiritually to heed Jesus' instruction; he received an overflow of blessings *(Luke 5:6, Matthew 25:1-13)*

# CHAPTER TWENTY ONE

# HUNGER AND THIRSTY FOR RIGHTEOUSNESS

All the Christian believers must strive to live a holy and righteous life at all times.

"Blessed are they which do hunger and thirst after righteousness: for they shall be filled," (Matthew 5:6).

"In the mean while his disciples prayed him, saying, Master, eat. But he said unto them, I have meat to eat that ye know not of; therefore, said the disciples one to another, Hath any man brought him ought to eat? Jesus said; unto them, my meat is to do the will of him that sent me, and to finish his work" (John 4:31-34)

Joseph was a classic example of someone who was hungry and thirsty for righteousness. He loved and feared the Lord. Even when sexual immorality was presented to him on a platter (with Potiphar's wife) with attendant benefits, he vehemently refused and said: *"How can I do this great wickedness, and sin against God?" (Genesis 39:9-10)*

Daniel was another classic example of someone who was both hungry and thirsty for righteousness. The Bible reveals that: Through under no obligation to live like a Rabbi, Daniel however felt no compulsion for self-indulgence like his Chaldean. It was on account of his thirst for righteousness that he determined not to be defiled himself with the royal rations of food and wine by eating with Chaldeans." *(Daniel chapter 1:8-21)*

The problem with many Christian Believers is the fact that they do not consider God worthy of their sacrifice of holiness. Such people miss the rewards of righteousness. The spirit of excellence is the reward for righteousness

The Bible says "Thou hast loved righteousness and hated iniquity; therefore, God even thy God, hath anointed thee with the oil of gladness above thy fellows" (Hebrews 1:9). This is excellence in action. Those who live righteously do not live in condemnation according to *Romans 8:1 which says. "There is therefore now no condemnation to them which are in Christ Jesus, who walk not after the flesh, but after the Spirit." (Romans 8:1)*

God is ready to grant all of humans heart desires if only they would first seek His righteousness *(Matthew 6:33).* All the Christian believers must pray that our Lord Jesus Christ let their heart be hunger and thirst for righteousness.

Brethren, whenever it pleases God to remember an individual, a family, a city, a nation or even the entire world, it is usually for divine intervention on rescue mission. It more often than not brings the opportunity of our cries to be heard by the Lord for His urgent and timely attention.

Really, nothing takes God by surprise and nothing happens accidentally before God. We should therefore bless the Lord and honor Him for His faithfulness over us, joyfully praising God, appreciating His Almightiness to display His mercy upon the whole Earth.

Our earthly knowledge, strength, skills, and technology may fail and disappointed us on this Earth, but God the Creator of heaven and Earth will never fail us or forsake us. God shall rescue us and grant us absolute victory to overcome any earthly problems.

The Lord visited Peter after he had toiled all night through and failed woefully. The Lord encouraged him that he refused to carry his outright failure on his head. Even when Jesus came; calling for the use of his boat, he did not advertise his failure and disappointment of the day by not releasing his boat when needed.

By this his attitude, his failure changed to instant outstanding success, the type that carries the glory of God and it was the glory of God that gave him victory all through his life.

No matter what disappointment, failure or labor loss you must have suffered, especially in the past be courageous, wait upon the Lord and He shall grant our life with divine touch for uncommon turn around fortunes that will bring great glory to His Holy Name.

Weeping and sorrowful moments shall give way to rejoicing, celebrations and jubilation in our life will radiate the glory of God from day-to-day we shall enjoy divine intervention in every area of our lives.

Apostle Paul said: *"So I am well pleased with weaknesses, with insults, with distresses, with persecutions, and with difficulties, for the sake of Christ; for when I am weak in human strength, then I am strong truly able, truly powerful, truly drawing from God's strength,"* (2 Corinthians 12:10).

And fear not them which kill the body, but are not able to kill the soul: but rather fear him which is able to destroy both soul and body in hell. *(Matthew 10:28)* Christian believers need strong faith: The kind of faith that tackles intimidation brings into manifestation the miracle- working power of God. Exodus 14:13 says:

*"And Moses said unto the people, Fear ye not, stand still, and see the salvation of the Lord, which he will show to you*

*Today: for the Egyptians whom ye have seen today, ye shall see them again no more forever."*

There will always be intimidating and doubtful situations, but we must continue to suppress the doubts with strong faith in God. This is where faith that thrives in the face of intimidation comes in.

In Mark 3:1-5, the Bible records that Jesus asked a man in a synagogue to stretch forth his hand, knowing fully well that it was withered. If that man had refused to act in great faith, he would have missed his miracle.

# CHAPTER TWENTY TWO

## SOLVING THE EARTHLY PROBLEMS WITH DIVINE WISDOM

And Pharaoh said unto his servant: "*Can we find such a one as this is, a man in whom the Spirit of God is? And Pharaoh said unto Joseph, Forasmuch as God hath showed thee all this, there is none so discreet and wise as thou art,*" (Genesis 41:38-40).

Divine wisdom of God equips a believer with the capacity for solution and answer to provision. Divine wisdom is the wisdom of God. One of the manifestations of Divine wisdom is that it connects people to solutions and answers to all sorts of problems and questions. The wisdom of God provides the keys to solve the mysteries of life.

The book of Genesis: We saw how Pharaoh dreamt a dream, but he had no interpretation. None of all the wise men and magicians of Egypt could interpret the dream until they found a man called Joseph. And Pharaoh's dream was not just a dream but a looming challenge – seven years of plenty that was going to be followed by seven years of famine. That was a situation that needed a practical solution. We saw how Joseph offered the solution by the wisdom of God.

So, the wisdom of God can make you offer solutions to the problems of a family, community, city, territory, nation, and even to a whole generation. The wisdom of God equips a person with the capacity for solution and answer provision.

Beloved, God is releasing His wisdom on you; you are becoming a problem solver. And it is possible that you are solving some problems around you now, but God is raising you to the realm of solving national, generational, territorial problems by the agency of His wisdom.

Remember this": The wisdom of God equips a person with the capacity for solution and answer provision. Joseph offered the solution by the wisdom of God and knowledge of God through suffering in his life. *(Genesis chapter 41:32-52)*

1. Live in the fear of the Lord. Let God's Word guide your actions and thoughts.

2. Do not just complain about the problems around you, trust God for wisdom to offer solutions.

We saw how Joseph offered the solution by the wisdom of God. So, the wisdom of God can make you offer solutions to the problems of a family, community, city, territory, nation, and even to a whole generation. The wisdom of God equips a person with the capacity for solution and answer provision.

## <u>AWARENESS OF COINCIDING WORDS OF LIFE</u>

MOSQUE is a six letter Word; CHURCH is a six letter Word. The First Two religions on Earth.

QUR'AN is a five letter word, same as the Bible, that is a five letter word.

Life is a four letter word; dead is a four letter word.

Love is a four letter word; hate is a four letter word.

Friends is a seven letter word; Enemies is also seven letter word.

Truth is a five letter word; Lying is also a five letter word.

Hurt is a four letter word; Heal is also four letter word

Positive is an eight letter word; Negative is also an eight letter word.

Success is a seven letter word; Failure is also a seven letter word.

Above are five letter words; Below is also five letter word.

Cry is three letter word; joy is a three letter word.

Anger is five letter word; happy is five letter word.

Right is a five letter word same is Wrong is five letter word.

Rich is a four letter word; poor is also four letter word.

Pass is a four letter word; fail is a four letter word.

Knowledge is nine letter word; ignorance is nine letter word.

Him is a three letter word; her is a three letter word.

Black is five letter word; white is a five letter word.

Table is a five letter word; chair is a five letter word.

Father is a six letter word; mother is also a six letter word.

Christian believers must be aware that our life is full of coincidences; therefore, life is like a clock ticking every minute, prayer is the Sword of the Holy Spirit that conquered the enemies; by His grace we are healed. All the believers will be divinely protected, defended, guarded, and delivered from any earthly troubles.

# CHAPTER TWENTY THREE

# IMPORTANT, EFFECTIVE, INSPIRATIONAL PSALMS FOR PRAYER

Psalms for help in time of trouble, Trial, Tribulations; Psalm 17, 25, 31, 61, 5, 2

Psalms In time of despair and struggling: Psalm 39, 42, 43, 55, 73, 77, 86, 88, 102, 130

Psalms for forgiveness from sin:  psalm 6, 32, 38, 51, 143, 145

Psalms to receive God's Goodness in prayer: Psalm 4, 11, 23, 27, 63, 67, 91, 115, 121, 125, 139

Psalms to Shout for Joy, praises, singing and thankfulness: Psalms 33, 47, 81, 66, 95, 98, 149, 150, 67, 103, 104

Psalms for God's Blessing to the nations in the world: Psalms 77, 68, 100, 108, 124, 126, 129,

Psalms to praise God for his awesome power and mercy: Psalms 8, 24, 29, 46, 50, 90, 93, 114, 145

Psalm for following God's Commandments: Psalms 19,119, 105, 118, 116, 77,

Psalms for God's creation of nature: Psalms 19, 65, 104, 105, 147, 148, 150

Psalms for Jesus Christ the Messiah: Psalms 2, 16, 22, 45, 69, 66, 89, 110, 132

Psalms for rebuilding the Temple in Jerusalem: Psalms 48, 84, 87, 122, 120

Psalms for the history of Israel and History of God Covenant 78, 105, 104, 106,

Psalms for War and Vindication Deliverance: Psalms 35, 58, 76, 79, 83, 109, 137, 139

Psalms for cry to God at the time of God's Anger of His People: Psalms 44, 74, 80, 85, 117,116,

Psalms for the fate of the wicked and the righteous: Psalms 1, 2, 15, 37, 49, 90

Psalm for prayer for God's personal Blessings upon His people: Psalms 18, 30, 34, 40, 65, 92, 103, 107, 105, 113, 116, 118, 146, 148

# CHAPTER TWENTY FOUR

## JESUS' TEACHING DURING HIS EARTHLY MINISTRY

The Gospel of Matthew chapter 5:1-12 (Beatitudes)

The teaching of the Bread of Life (John chapter 6:25-59)

Teaching about Nicodemus you must be born again: (John 3; 1-22)

To discipleship: (Luke 14:25-35)

Teaching of give to Caesar what belongs to Caesar: (Mark 12:13-17)

The teaching of the Good Shepherd (John chapter 10; 1- 21)

The teaching about the Golden Rule (Luke chapter 6:31)

The teaching about the great God's Commandment (Matthew 22:34-40)

Teaching about the Living Water (John Chapter 4: 1-26)

The teaching of our Lord and how we must pray: (Matthew 6:5-15)

Teaching and the example of the Great Commission by sending the Twelve disciples out (Matthew chapter 10)

Teaching about the Sermon on the Mount (Matthew chapter five to chapter 7)

Teaching about the Vine and the Branches (John chapter 15:1-17)

Teaching of Jesus been the Way the Truth and The Life: (John Chapter 14:5-14)

Teaching about the rich and the poor storing up wealth on Earth: (Matthew Chapter 19:16-30)

Christ teaching about worriedness: (Luke chapter 12:22-34)

# CHAPTER TWENTY FIVE

## JESUS CHRIST TEACHES AND PREACHES IN PARABLES

Parable of the Talent (Matthew chapter 25 14-30 )

Parable of Tenants (Matthew 21:33-34; Mark 12:1-11; Luke 20:9-18)

Parable of Ten Minas (Luke Chapters 19:12-27)

Parables of two sons:  (Matthew 21; 28-32)

Parable of unforgiving servant: (Matthew 18; 23-35)

Parable of the unfruitful fig tree:  (Luke 13:6-9)

Parable of Wedding Banquet: (Matthew 22:2-14)

Parable of Watchful slaves: (Mark 13:34-37; Luke chapter 12: 35-40)

Parable of weeds and Tares (Matthew 13:24-30, 36-43)

*Parable of the Weeds and the Tares in the book of Matthew our Lord Jesus Christ explained  clearly to the disciples that: "The Kingdom of God is like a man who sowed good seed in his field. But while everyone was sleeping his enemy came and sowed weeds among the wheat, and went away. When the wheat sprouted and formed heads, then the weeds also appeared. The owner's servants came to him and said , 'Sir, didn't you sow good seed in your field? Where then did the weeds come from?' 'An enemy did this,' he replied. The servant asked him, 'Do you want us to go and pull them up?' 'No,' he answered, 'because while you are pulling the weeds, you may root up the wheat with them. Let both grow together until the harvest. At that time I will tell the harvesters: First collect the weeds and tie them in bundles to be burned; then gather the wheat and bring it into my barn.' " (Matthew 13:24-30)*

Parable of wise and foolish builders (Matthew chapter 7:24-27, Luke chapter 6:47-49)

Parable of Yeast (Matthew chapter 13:33; Luke chapter 13:20-2)

Parable of Sower (Matthew chapter 13; 1-8, 18-23; Mark 4:3-9, 14-20; Luke 8:5-8, 11-15)

Parable of Shrewd manager (Luke chapter 16:1-8)

Parable of the Sheep and the Goats (Matthew chapter 25:31-46)

Parable of Rich man and Lazarus (Luke chapter 16:19-31)

Parable of Rich Fool (Luke chapter 12:16-21)

Parable of prodigal son (Luke chapter 15:11-32)

Parable of Pharisee and the tax collector (Luke chapter 18:10-14)

Parable of the Mustard Seed (Matthew chapter 13:31-31 mark 4:30-32; Luke 13: 18-19)

Parable of New wine in old wineskins (Matthew chapter 9:17, Mark 2; 22, Luke 5:37-39)

Parable of laborers in the vineyard (Matthew chapter 20:1-16)

Parable of Hidden treasure and the pearl (Matthew chapter 12; 44-46)

Parable of the Good Samaritan (Luke chapter 10; 30-37)

Parable of the Faithful Servant (Matthew chapter 24:45-51; Luke 12:42-48)

Cost of discipleship (Luke chapter 14:28-33)

Parable of canceled debts (Luke chapter 76:41-43)

Parable of the Fig Tree (Mathew chapter 24; 32-35; Mark chapter 13; 28-31; Luke chapter 21:29-39)

Parable of Honor at a Banquet (Luke chapter 14:7-14)

Parable of The great Dinner (Luke chapter 14:16-24)

Parable of light in the world (Matthew chapter 5:14-16; mark 4; 30- 4:21-22; Luke 8:16; 11:33-36)

Parable of Lost Coin (Luke chapter 15:8-110)

Parable of Owner of the House (Matthew chapter 13:52)

Parable of the persistent friend (Luke chapter 11:5-8)

Parable of the Persistent Widow (Luke chapter 18:2-9)

Parable of Net (Matthew chapter 13:47-50)

Parable of New Clothe on an old garment (Matthew chapter 9:16; Mark 2; 21; Luke chapter 5:36)

Parable of the shrewd manager (Luke chapter 16:1-8 )

Parable of the Sower (Matthew chapter 13:1-8; Mark 4:3-9; 14-20; Luke 8:5-9, 11-15)

# CHAPTER TWENTY SIX

## PROPRER PRAYER POSTURE

A Christian's proper prayer posture is not the position of our body; it is the position of our heart and a humble spirit. It is about humility. Our position during prayer helps us to pray in the power of the Holy Spirit. Here are some suggested postures for prayer.

(1)      <u>Prayer On Our Knee</u>: Denotes total surrender to the Lord God Almighty. King Solomon's prayer of supplication during the dedication of the Temple; kneeling with his hands spread out towards heaven. King Solomon's prayer is an ideal model for what we Christians should desire in our walk with the Lord – 1st Kings 8:54-61. Our Lord prays at Mount Olives. He withdrew about a stone throw from his disciples, kneeling down and prayed – Luke 22:39-46; Apostle Peter sent all the people out, he got down on his knees and prayed, turning towards the dead woman Tabitha, and Tabitha woke up, opened her eyes - Act 9:36-43 Apostle Paul's prayer for the Ephesians, he said, "For this reason I Kneel before the Father; asking to be strengthened by the Spirit; for God's love in His Son Jesus Christ to have a deep root and grow strong with foundations and land on a solid rock – Ephesians 3:14-21

(2)      Pray While Laying On Your Bed: The word of the Lord says, "In your anger do not sin, when you are on your bed – meditate within your heart on your bed and be still, be silent  be of a quiet spirit." – Psalm 4:4-5

(3)      Cry Out Loud: We cry out loud to the Lord in prayer to extol the Lord God Almighty. He hears the prayers of those who fear Him, and they lack nothing.  God has appointed His angels to protect and rescue His Saints from physical and spiritual harm; His divine intervention is reserved for those who truly and sincerely love Him – Psalm 34:1-22

(4)      Pray Silently: Means praying in our heart to the Lord without opening our mouth.  Hannah showed her gratitude, love and devotion to the Lord while she was praying in the Temple; she wept and prayed saying: "O Lord God Almighty if you give me a child I will dedicate the child to your service" – 1st Samuel 1:10-18

(5)      Praying With Hands Lifted High: Lifting up hands is a position of praise, acknowledgement and a place of surrender praying with lifted hands is a sign of confidently approaching the throne room of God.  King Solomon stood before the alter of the Lord in front of the whole assembly spread out his hands in prayer – 2nd Chronicles 6:12-42 ; Apostle Paul told Timothy that all people everywhere to lift up holy hands in prayer. It is customary for worshipers to lift their hands and offer prayers aloud, because for our prayers to be effective; we must pray with Holy Hands which represent clean, Holy and Righteous lives – 1st Timothy 2:1-15

(6)      Praying With Eyes Open: Praying with eyes open is very effective in prayers as our Lord prayed a

priestly prayer for Himself and for all believers and He looked toward heaven and prayed final prayer for His disciples and all those who will believe on Him until He returns.  Looking up to heaven He prayed for eternal life and for obeying His Word. – John 17:1-26

(7)	<u>Head Bowed Down</u>:  Moses bowed down to the ground at once to worship and pray – Exodus 34:8-28; In another Scripture we see "Bowed down" in prayer. Scripture says: "All Kings will bow down to the Lord and all nations will serve Him" – Psalm 72:11-19; Another Scripture says, "Then the man bowed down and worshiped the Lord; bowing down in prayer is a sign of total submission to the Lord.  In the book of Nehemiah, Ezra praised the Lord, the great God bowed down and worshiped, and it was one of the greatest worship services of all time. Bowed down displays spirit of humility; God Almighty desires the adoration of His people and calls them to worship Him regularly – Nehemiah 8:6-11

(8)	<u>Prostrate In Prayer</u>: Prostrate shows an awe of the holiness of God a position of crying out to God, a position of repentance and total surrender. Ezra was praying and confessing, weeping, and throwing himself down before the Lord. True repentance from knowing and unknown sins requires prostrating posture prayer.  Ezra was grieved over Israel's spiritual sins in front of the great assembly – Ezra 10: 1-18 In another  Scripture Joshua tore his clothes and fell facedown to the ground before the ark of the Lord – Joshua 7:6-15; In the Garden of Gethsemane our Lord Jesus Christ fell down with his face to the ground and prayed, *"My Father if it is possible ... "* Our Lord prayed that His physical death might be accepted as the full payment for the sins of sinners -  Matthew 26:39; Mark 14:35-42

(9)     Prayer Standing Up: When you are standing up praying – it is a position of forgiveness.  All Christians must not carry or hold secretly, bitterness in their hearts against anyone If you– *Mark 11:25-26*; "If your brother sins against you, you must forgive him, …", which includes all the Church members – *Matthew 18:15-21*

*(10)*     Praying Sitting: King David's prayer; He went in and sat before the Lord and said, "Whom am I, Lord God…" It is a position of humility for God's grace, not his own merit.  He was successful and with God's covenant – *1ˢᵗ Chronicles 17:16-27*

(11)     Praying Looking Up To Heaven: Demonstrates where our help comes from – Our help comes from God, the only source for meeting our needs physically and spiritually.  We must trust the Lord with all our hearts and seek Him for grace to help in our time of need; His protection, defense and watchful care – *Psalm 121:1-8* another Scripture: So they took away the stone, Jesus looked up to heaven and said: "Father, I thank you that you always hear me…" The dead man came out of the grave.  Our Lord woke up Lazarus from the grave after four days "Lazarus Come Out" – *John 11:40-44;* another Scripture says: After Jesus said this, he looked toward heaven and prayed, "Father, the time has come glorify your Son, that your Son may glorify you…" *John 17:1-26.* Our Lord gave us the example of praying with confidence by looking up toward heaven in most of His earthly prayers.

(12)     Praying Walking:  Elisha turned away and walked back and forth in the room and then got on the bed

and stretched out upon him once more.  The boy sneezed seven times and opened his eyes. Elisha was walking to and fro in the room where the boy lay dead and prayed to God to bring the child back to life – *2nd Kings 4:35-37* When we are walking praying, we are waging war against the enemies of God.

Praying Boldly: Is a position of humbleness in spirit, soul, and body.  The book of Hebrews says: "Let us therefore, approach the throne of grace with boldness with confidence because Jesus Christ sympathizes with our weaknesses, we can confidently approach the heavenly throne knowing that our prayers and petitions are welcomed and desired by our heavenly Father."  Also called the throne of grace because from it flows God's love, help, mercy, forgiveness, wisdom, spiritual power, spiritual gifts, the fruit of the Holy Spirit and all that we need in any circumstances – Hebrew 4:16

Summarization: The standing position of forgiveness to others means that our Father in heaven will forgive us of known and unknown sins.  Praying with hands lifted high up is a sign of confidently approaching the throne room of God.  King Solomon stand before the Altar of the Lord in front of the whole assembly spread out his hands in prayer.

Apostle Paul told Timothy that all people everywhere to lift up holy hands in prayer.  It is a customary for worshipers to lift their hands and offer prayers aloud; because for our prayers to be effective we must pray with holy hands, which represent clean, holy, and righteous lives.

Praying with your eyes open is very effective in prayer as our Lord prayed His priestly prayer for Himself and for all believers; He looked toward heaven and prayed final prayer for His disciples and all those who will believe on Him until He returns back to Earth, as He looked up to heaven for eternal life and obey His Word.

<u>Head bowed down</u> - Moses bowed to the ground at once to worship and pray. In another Scripture, we see bowed down in prayer that says all Kings will bow down to the Lord and all nations will serve Him, and we see where a man bowed down and worshiped the Lord bowing down is prayer is a sign of total submission to the Lord.

In the book Nehemiah, Ezra praised the Lord, the great God and bowed down and worshiped, it was one of the greatest worship services. Bowed down displays humility at all times. God Almighty desires the adoration of His people and calls them to worship Him regularly. Prostrate in prayer while Ezra was praying and confession, weeping and throwing himself down before the Lord demonstrate true repentance required separation for rectify evil.

<u>Kneeling down to pray</u> is one of the most common positions of prayer by all the believers The Scripture revealed: "Before me every knee will bow, by me and every tongue will swear." Isaiah 45:23; "Come, let us bow down in worship, let us kneel before the Lord our Maker," Psalm 95:6. Every knee shall bow down; shows that although not every person turns to the Lord in true repentance, in this life, but all people will one day, either voluntarily or involuntarily, will bow before Jesus Christ to confess that He is the Lord of and Savior of all.

Apostle Paul said: "For this reason I kneel before the Father, from whom his whole family in heaven and on earth derives its name." Ephesians 3:14. It is position spiritually mature in fullness of Christ spiritually mature means that we presented our prayers with truth, understanding, commitment with love that is in Christ Jesus our Lord.

Many people prostrate in prayer for complete repentance from known and unknown sins. Ezra was grieved over Israel's spiritual sins in front of the great assembly. In another Scripture, Joshua tore his clothes and fell faced down to the ground before the Ark of the Lord. Our Lord and Savior of all the people on Earth; in the Garden of Gethsemane, Jesus, fell down with His face to the ground and prayed.

Our Lord Jesus Christ prayed that He should be strengthened and that His physical death might be accepted as full payment for the sin of the whole world.

Prostrate is a sign of revival among God's people; it shows an awe of the holiness of God. it is a position of crying out to God, a position of repentance and total surrender. Walking or warring position begins to stir up your prayer's intensity; thus it is hard to sit while at war, this makes you come boldly to approach the throne of God with humbleness of prayer. While lifting up hands is a position of praise, acknowledgement of a place of sound prayer. While standing when praying is a position of forgiveness. All Christians must not carry or hold secretly, bitterness in their hearts against anyone; if your brother sin against you, you must forgive him. It includes all the church members.

Sitting - King David always sit before the lord to pray it is a position of humility for God's grace, not his own merit he was successful; because of God's covenant with King David. Looking up to heaven demonstrates where our help comes from - our help comes from God the only source of all things that meeting our needs physically and spiritually. We must trust the Lord with all our hearts and seek Him for His grace to help in our time of needs; protection, defense and for His watchful care.

The scripture revealed that they took away the stone -- Jesus the Lord and giver of life looked up to heaven and prayed and thanked God the Father for listening to His prayer; and for answering all His prayers after he called Lazarus out of the grave after four days in the tomb. Our Lord the giver of all life wakes up Lazarus from the grave Jesus Christ looked towards heaven. All Christian believers must copy the model of our Lord's Prayer. Christ gave us the example of praying with confidence by looking up to heaven in most of His earthly prayers.

Our proper prayer posture is not the position of our body; it is the position of our heart and humble spirit. It is about humility.

Walking praying like Elisha turned around back and forth, to and fro, in the room and then continues in the same prayer mode until the boy sneezed seven times and come back to life. By walking praying we are waging war against the enemies of God. Helping us to pray boldly is a position of humbleness in spirit, soul, and body.

The Scripture revealed in the book of Hebrew: *"Let us therefore approach the throne of grace with boldness so that we may receive mercy and find grace to help in time of need" (Hebrew 4:16)* Christians should approach the throne of grace with confidence because Jesus Christ sympathizes with our weaknesses, we can confidently approach the heavenly throne knowing that our prayers and petitions are welcomed and desired by our heavenly Father.  Also called the throne of grace because from it flow God's love, help, mercy, forgiveness, wisdom, spiritual power, spiritual gifts, the fruit of the spirit; and all that we need in any circumstance.

# CHAPTER TWENTY SEVEN

## THE JOURNEY OF LIFE

The journey of life begins from fifty years old, sixty years old, seventy years, eighty years, ninety years, one hundred years - all the years started from day one when we arrived on this Earth from the worm of our mother. We cannot know how long we are going to live on this Earth; all we know is the journey is too short for everyone; rich, poor, and middle-class. Therefore, we must thank God the Father, Son, and the Holy Spirit for the years we have to spend on this Earth up to the last minute and second. We must value the people around us and cherish them when we are still on Earth.

We must Love God Almighty for the gift of life every day when we wake up in the morning to see a new day, new month, New Year. We must not offend anyone, and most importantly, we must have a mind and heart of forgiveness without carrying bitterness and grudges within us as we do not know when we are going to leave this world. Always remember that the journey of life is too short; never forget to say your prayer in the morning and at night. Let the Word of God be the first in your mouth when you wake up and let the Word of God be the last word in your mouth before you sleep at night. We should not let anyone break our heart. We must be calm because the journey is short. If anyone betrays you, cheats, or humiliates you, even screams and yells at you, be very calm, forgive the person because the journey is too short. You need your peace of mind. Let us be full of gratitude and sweetness. Sweetness is the key to life; never allow bad character to rule your life - be great, with greatness, the journey will be full of happiness. No one know the duration of the journey of life. We must pray for long life and prosperity in order to be able to fulfill the will of God and His purpose for our life on this Earth. No one knows the last day, time, and hour.

Pastors, ministers, prophets & prophetesses, they are very special, but some of them are fake and do not know the Lord. Our Lord Said in the Holy Scripture: *"But he will say, I do not know where you come from; go away from me, all you evildoers!" (Matthew 7:23)* Most of the Pastors base their ministry strictly on Tithes and Offerings; if you are a poor person you will not be comfortable in their church. Some pastors place price tags on counseling the congregation, rule their homes and their personal life. We have to know that not all the pastors are servants of God. They are a money ministry church; some will tell you or to put in the offering as the Lord provides for you. Congregations are more comfortable in a church with a pastor like that. Some of the pastors take advantage of people's needs, and perform scary miracles to deceive the people who are sick, disabled, barren, or in trouble. The worst of the pastors are the ones that are sexually immoral and sexually assault women in their church; even if they know they are married. Some pastors are very proud to the people in their church; they feel that you cannot talk to them without an appointment. They don't care what type of emergency the person is going through; those are very lazy, but they cover their laziness with pride. The worst ones are the pastors seeking power from an evil spirit and demons. There are some pastors that have called themselves shepherds; there is no fear of God in their heart, some of them are Herbalists joining the work of darkness with the Word of God. All ministers, pastors, servants of God who own their own church are denomination sales pastors; they will tell the congregation to buy houses, and invest their money through the church. The worst behavior of some pastors is that they seek fame by any means, on the news media, they do not use the offering money for the work of God. They pile it up in their own bank account, living in luxury, riding in $65million dollar airplanes, living in a 50 million dollar mansions, while they continue screaming at the poor congregation for not paying the Tithe and Offering. Our Lord Jesus Christ knows whom He called to serve Him, and those that He did not call, they know also that He did not call them to them to a ministry that is a multi-million dollar business evangelism. Our Lord said that we have to know that there are fake pastors, ministers, just as there are fake medical doctors, nurses, professors, and technicians.

The Scripture revealed: *"Apostle told the Lord, 'Master, we saw someone casting out demons in your name, and we tried to stop him, because he does not follow with us. But Jesus said to him.' 'Do not stop him for whoever is not against you is for you' (Luke 9:49-50) NIV.* There also fake Christians; they go to church every Sunday, participate in church services, as an elder, deacons, or those who are taking care of financial services of the church, but never are a Christian, stealing some of the offering money of the church in the thousands and millions. The fact is that only God knows who belongs to Him.

## Coincidence of Words

On this Earth we have so many, many words that were coincidence of this life; we need place close attention. These are the list of some of coincidences words that we need to know and pay close attention.  They have the same letter words; we should know that God authored them to be this way:

**Qur'an is five letters words and Bible is the same five letter words.**

**Life has four letters same as Dead. Church is of six letters the same as Mosque.**

**We have the word Father with six letters same as the word Mother has six letter words.**

**Love has four letters words same as Hate.**

**What about Friends contains seven letter words as Enemies.**

**Let us look as lying it has five letters words same as Truth.**

**What about Positive eight letters words same as Negative. Hurt has four letters same as Heal.**

**We have the word Success has seven letters same as Failure.**

**We have the word Cry with three letters same as three letters as Joy.**

**We have Above which has the five letters word as Below.**

**We have the word Right which has five letters same as Wrong.**

**We have Happy which is five letters same as Anger with five letter words.**

**We have the word Rich which has four letter words as Poor.**

**We have the word Him with three letters and Her with three letter words.**

**We have the word Pass with four letters with the same as Fail.**

**We have the word White with five letters words same as Black.**

**We have the word Knowledge with nine letter word same as Ignorance with the same nine letter words.**

**We have the word Table with five letter words as Chair.**

All these words are coincidence, means life is more than what we think it to be; we should also think of our own words and behavior: For example when we Laugh, we make people around us laugh, even if they are going through some sadness. It is the same as when we are rich and when we distribute the success, to serve others and other people serve us. Perhaps their life get better with the Job they received from us. In order to be prospering, we must be an honest person; in order to be excelling to the top, we must be a faithful person in everything we do in our lives. In order to make it to the top we have to work hard and go very far, get up early in the morning and work. In order to change someone we must set an example by changing our self-first, so that other people around us will follow. In order to be a great person we must be able to discipline our self, making our self-strong and most importantly, we must pray without ceasing. In order to live in peace, we must listen carefully, and speak very little in every situation. To be able to bear fruit, we must get close to the Lord God and praise His Holy name. Also, in order to live a holy live we must have mind of forgiveness, and get rid of all anger and bitterness, and talk to people in a well behavior. In order to have a good sleep at night, we must work hard to clear our mind and heart in our life.  In order to be love, we must show our love to other people around us.  In order to be a good father and a good husband, you must listen to your children and your wife.  Also, a woman must listen to her husband and submit herself to the correction of her husband.  If you want people to respect you, you must be very polite.  Bind Satan from all the areas of your lives by sanctifying yourself with Word of God and the power of the Holy Spirit.  Christians that want to be grow in faith and sanctification must be able to meditate on the daily Word of God with prayer. We also must be able to give to others who are in need.

# CHAPTER TWENTY EIGHT

## THE CROSS OF JESUS CHRIST

The meaning of the Cross as revealed in God's purpose. God almighty Father mentioned the Cross in the book of Isaiah seven hundred years before its fulfillment. God saw that it was the only solution for the redeeming of human being from sin and death. Jesus Christ paid it all. He purchased us with His precious blood on the Calvary tree. God's infinite love is manifested in the Universe. The Cross of Jesus Christ is the cross of love, the cross of mercy of God the Father Almighty to the people of this Earth.

The Cross of Jesus is the cross of great compassion, the cross of Jesus is the power of God the Father, God the Son, and God the Holy Spirit. The Cross of Jesus is the cross of peace to the world, the cross of promise of eternal life to mankind; the Cross of fulfillment of deliverance from sin and death. The Cross of the goodness of God the Father Almighty, the cross of knowledge, the cross of kindness, the cross of humbleness, the cross of justification, cross of the wisdom of God. The Cross of Christ is the cross of communion with the Trinity, the cross of total surrender to the lordship of Jesus Christ. The Cross of Jesus is the cross of sanctification, cross of justification, cross of magnification, cross of salvation, cross of sinners and the lost, the cross of Jesus is the message to the people of the world. The cross of the new heaven and a new earth.  The Cross of Christ Jesus is the cross of glory of God, the cross of worship in  spirit and in truth. The Cross of Jesus is the cross of truth, the cross of a new life in Jesus Christ; the Cross of Jesus is the cross of forgiveness, the cross of righteousness, the cross of adoration, the cross of grace.  The Cross of Jesus is the cross of light to the world in the darkness.  On the Cross we first saw the Lord and all our sins rolled away.  The cross of Christ is the cross of blessing of the Holy Trinity forever one God.  The cross of Christ is the cross of faithfulness, the cross of perfect obedience to the Lord God Almighty. The Cross of Jesus is the cross of long suffering for the people of this Earth.  The Cross of Jesus is the cross of New Covenant from God; the Cross of Jesus is the cross of message of peace to the world of sin.  It is on the cross where the Son of God was crucified.  On the cross of Christ our salvation is completed, our Lord Jesus Christ said, *"It is Finished," (Luke 23:46-47)* and the work of redemption was completed.  If Jesus Christ did not go to the Cross, there would be no remission of sins, resurrection of the body, and life everlasting. Amen! Amen! Amen!

# CHAPTER TWENTY NINE

## FIRST THING TO DO WHEN YOU WAKE UP

Acknowledge God - Praise His Holy Name for waking you up in the morning to another day; praise Him for the gift of life, thank him for his grace and mercy and His unfailingly love for you and your entire family.  Give thanks to the Lord Jesus Christ at all times for your life, and appreciate what the Lord is doing in your life and what He is still going to do in your life. Read Scripture, such as Psalm 24, 27, and your Daily Devotional for the day.  Pray, make yourself clean from sins, knowing and unknown sins, do not engage in any work of evil or destruction, be holy in all your dealings in the office, and in all the areas of your life throughout the day.  Put in your prayer: To be divinely protected and triumph over all your work of the day. To be Delivered from all form evil of the day and all the days of your life, Ask for strength for Success in all your endeavors for the day; Ask to be Highly favored in all your business and on your work be prosper in all the areas of your life. Ask for God's protection that the wind of destruction will not come to your dwelling place.  Pray that you will overcome all the obstacles of life physically and spiritually.  Ask for comfort from God of all Comfort. Ask the Lord's divine help in everything you are doing and going to do, ask for His dealing throughout your life.  Pray that the Lord fight your battles, afflictions, tribulations, and rescue you from all evil and from the work of the enemy.  Ask the Lord Jesus Christ to uphold you in his Holy Hands.  Pray that you do not labor in vain in all the areas of your lives.  Pray for the empowerment of the Holy Spirit in all your life, with unlimited out pouring of His blessings. Pray that the Lord return all what the enemy took away from you in hundred fold.  Ask for His Divine presence at all time in your life. Ask for help in all the nations of Earth.  Pray that you will be divinely lifted above all principalities and powers of the enemy by the power of the Holy Spirit.  Ask that the Holy Spirit open your spiritual eye to see what is going on in your life and grant you with wisdom, knowledge and understanding of the Scripture that you read every day. The Scripture stated be Holy For I am Holy.  Stay in the Word of God by putting the Word of God in your heart.  Ask the Lord Jesus Christ to take total control of your day.

### The Encourager

The Encourager: The Encouragers keep people that are going through discouragement in their life, help them physically and spiritually with the Word of God pray that you meet them at time of your struggles.

The Destiny Helper: are the people that provide and help you to fulfill your dream and work on your goal that the Lord assigned for you to follow.  We need them in our life.

There are some people they call them the Hand Lifter.  They are those who are strong enough to help you in time of your weakness; pray that you meet them in time of your need.

The givers are those people work very hard and always ready to give their time, talent, money, treasure to someone who are in need; they can provide shelter, food money, etc.

There are some people called the receivers in time of financial disaster, they are different from beggars.  You can help them by given them a job, clothing, or praying for them, as you help them, they will return what you give with an abundant blessings to you.  Pray that you will meet them.

There are people called the Prayer Conqueror many people like that pray for from their hearts and mind in order to conquer the problem of the people we need them in our lives.  Then we have some people called Recommender, they will mention name to the people who can help you with your talent, and your business.

We have people called the corrector; these people are the one who honestly talk to you advise you if you do anything, or wanted to do anything that can hurt your life, and your dream life.  The Committed people are the people who are fully committed to the work of the Lord whether things are going good or not, these people will stand with you in trouble, afflictions, and in any form of trouble you might be going through in your life. We have people that were very Loyal with people around them; they work with you with their heart and mind in order to make sure that your life is better.

The Truth Teller are the people that always tell the truth of all that is going on in this life.  They will not tell you what is wrong or make up stories in order to gain your love.  The Altruist is the people that believe that the life is not about them alone and is about everyone on Earth.  They live a simple life of peace.

The Contented people are one of the best people in the world;  they are content with what they have.  They will fight for what belongs to them, and they will not try to get what belongs to anyone around them.  They live in contentment and a life of peace.  The other people are the Lover and pursuers of God and a godly life.  These people are the pursuer of holy and godly life at all times; they always connect with the Holy Trinity forever one God and never do anything that can disconnect from their life.  We need to pray in order to meet them.

Divine Wisdom is the wisdom of God the Father Almighty and one of the manifestations of divine wisdom is that it connects people to solve the problem solutions and find answers to the problems; the wisdom of God provides the key that makes the mysteries of life clearer and simple to understand what we are going through in life.

## The Power of Our Thoughts

The quality of our thought determines the quality of our life, our thought affects the quality of our dreams in life and our destiny. The quality of our thought also determines the quality of our answers to what we are going through in life. The Scripture revealed, *"Keep your heart with all vigilance, for from it flow the springs of life; let your eyes look directly forward, and your gaze be straight before you," (Proverbs 4: 23, 25 NIV).*  The mind of some people full of evil thoughts, pride, and destruction, sins, thought is very powerful in the life of human being.

One of the powerful weapons of life is our thoughts. Thoughts can destroy life. Thoughts can create a war between nations, thoughts can make a life difficult for the entire nation or make life easier , thoughts can raise a life, and thoughts also ruin the life of self and all other people around them. Thoughts can help someone to make it to heaven by preaching the Gospel to them, and show them the way of salvation.  Thoughts can also lead people to prison, and to hell.  Thoughts can bring great blessings to the entire world; thoughts have also brought the greatest problems to the entire world.

An example of Napoleon, the Greek Empire; Adolph Rudolf Hitler Second World War, where six million Jews perished.  People perished because all began from bad and wicked, selfish thoughts.  The Scripture stated: *"The mouth of the righteous is a fountain of life, but the mouth of the wicked conceals violence. Hatred stirs up strife,"* (Proverbs 10:11-12a).  "The good person out of the good treasure of the heart produces good, and the evil person out evil treasure produces evil; for it is out of the abundance of the heart that the mouth speaks," (Luke 6:45).  Thoughts determined the result of everything we do in our life.  Our thoughts surely determines the quality, which affect the result of our destiny.  Our life cannot rise up above the level of our thoughts.  Our life is where our thoughts brought us.  Thought has permitted us to be where we wanted to be, our thoughts determines our destiny, and our future.  Those who are on drugs constantly; it is because their thoughts are on drugs, and continue going to use it again and again even though they know that it is destroying their life.

All the Christians must stay in the Word of God in other to upgrade their thoughts in order to change their destiny, and follow their dreams with the help of God.  We must upgrade our thoughts consistently by meditating on the Word of God, and prayer.  Do not put your thoughts on earthly things such as immoralities.  Totally surrender your thoughts to the hands of the Lord Jesus Christ and tell him to take total care of your thought every day of your life.  Thoughts are very powerful in the life of every human being; we must let God control our thoughts.  Our thoughts creates action and action determines the result of our life.

# CHAPTER THIRTY

## PERSECUTION, SUFFERING & FRUIT OF THE HOLY SPIRIT

All the Christian believers must be able to welcome suffering in their life; Christians go through persecution every day in all forms of life; from the early Christian era to the present. This is how each apostle were persecuted and died:

1.  Matthew suffered martyrdom in Ethiopia, killed by a sword wound.

2.  Mark died in Alexandria, Egypt , after being dragged by Horses through the streets until he was dead.

3.  Luke was hanged in Greece as a result of his tremendous preaching to the lost.

4  Peter was crucified upside down on an X-shaped cross.

According to Church tradition it was because he told his tormentors that he felt unworthy to die In the same way that Jesus Christ had died.

5.  James , the leader of the Church in Jerusalem , was thrown over a hundred feet down from the southeast pinnacle of the Temple when he refused to deny his faith in Christ. When they discovered that he survived the fall, his enemies beat James to

death with a fuller's club.  This was the same pinnacle where Satan had taken Jesus during the Temptation.

6   James  (the Son of Zebedee)  was a fisherman by trade when Jesus called him to a lifetime of ministry.  As a strong leader of the Church, James was  beheaded at Jerusalem.  The Roman officer who guarded James watched amazed as James defended his faith at his trial.  Later, the officer walked beside James to the place of execution.  Overcome by conviction, he declared his new faith to the judge and knelt beside James to accept beheading as a Christian.

7.   Bartholomew , Also known as Nathaniel, was a missionary to Asia.  He witnessed for our Lord in present day Turkey.  Bartholomew was martyred for his preaching in Armenia where he was flayed to death by a whip.

8.   Andrew  Was crucified on an x-shaped cross in Patras, Greece.  After being whipped severely by seven soldiers they tied his body to the cross with cords to prolong his agony.  His followers reported that, when he was led toward the cross, Andrew saluted it in these words:  "I have long desired and expected this happy hour. The cross has been consecrated by the body of Christ hanging on it. " He continued to preach to his tormentors for two days until he expired.

9.   Thomas Was stabbed with a spear in India during one of his missionary trips to establish the church in the Sub-continent.

10.   Jude was killed with arrows when he refused to deny his faith in Christ.

11.   Matthias, the apostle chosen to replace the traitor Judas Iscariot was stoned and then beheaded.

12.    Paul was tortured and then beheaded by the evil Emperor Nero at Rome in A.D. 67.  Paul endured a lengthy imprisonment, which allowed him to write his many epistles to the churches he had formed throughout the Roman Empire.

13    John faced martyrdom when he was boiled in huge Basin of boiling oil during a wave of persecution in Rome. However, he was miraculously delivered from death.  John was then sentenced to the mines on the prison Island of Patmos.  He wrote his prophetic Book of Revelation on Patmos.  The apostle John was later freed and returned to serve as Bishop of Edessa in modern Turkey.  He died as an old man, the only apostle to die peacefully.

This must remind us of the foundational Doctrines of Christianity from Old Testament to the New Testament.  It is also, to alert all the Christians on Earth that sufferings, persecution afflictions, tribulations, trials and struggling are part of being a Christian and Children of God.  The Apostles during their time faced and go through serious persecution, cruelty, hatred for their faith but they never denied their Lord; and their faith was never shaky. The Scripture revealed: *"Blessed are those who are persecuted for righteousness sake, for theirs is the kingdom of heaven. Blessed are you when people revile you and persecute you and utter all kinds of evil against you falsely on my account.  Rejoice and be glad, for your reward is great in heaven, for in the same way they persecuted the prophets who were before you,"* (Matthew 5:10-11).

Persecution because of righteousness will be the lot of all who seek to life in harmony with God's Word for the sake of righteousness.  Those who uphold God's standards of the, justice and purity, at the same time refused to compromise with the present evil society of lifestyles of lukewarm believers will undergo unpopularity, rejection, and criticism. Persecution and opposition will come from the world and at times from those within the professing church.  When Christian experience suffering, they should rejoice for to those who suffer most, God imparts the highest blessing.  All Christians must be aware of the temptation to compromise God's will in order to avoid shame, embarrassment, or loss.  The principles of God's kingdom will never change.  Everyone who wants to live a godly life in Jesus Christ will be persecuted. Those who suffer and endure persecution because of righteousness are promised the Kingdom and heavenly rewards.

# SUMMARY

Prayer is a communication with God the Father Almighty, Jesus Christ, His only Son, and the Holy Spirit forever one God; it as well as an intercession.  Moses most famous prayer in the book of *Numbers, Chapter 10:35-36; 6:22-27.*

The model of prayer of King Jehoshaphat's prayer and victory in the book of *2nd Chronicles chapter 20:5-30,* King Jehoshaphat will begin his prayer with adoration of God, by reminding God of his promises, he will narrated his problems and ask for God's help confidently; and then give thanks to God for answering his prayer even before he receive what he asked for came through.

King Solomon's prayer of dedication in the book of *1st Kings chapter 8:22-30,* he made it clear that the God of the Earth cannot fully dwell in a building; God's presence, or his name, he prayed toward Jerusalem a practice that is still followed by many Israelites up till today.

Nehemiah model of Arrow Prayer: Nehemiah prays ceaselessly to God while he was working in the King palace in exile.  The characteristic of his prayer was so different - showing an arrow to God; silently, queasily asking God for help in the middle of his conversation with the King.  He continuously inserted prayers in his memoirs: The book of Nehemiah chapter 1:5-11; 2:4; 4:9 , 4:4-

5; 5:19; 6:9,14; 13:14-22; 31; prayer of oppression; stained glass prayer chapter 9:6

Ezekiel's prayer: Bones in the valley which means the renewal of Israelites: the book of Ezekiel Chapter 36:16-38; 37:1-14; referred to the book of Genesis 2, 7; where God breathed life into Adam. The book of Ezekiel chapter 20:3 during Israel's rebellion to God, God said they should not ask him anything in prayer until they change their rebellious behavior character.

Daniel's prayer chapter 6:16-28 Daniel's remarkable prayer for the people that expresses his intimate relationship with God: In the book of Daniel chapter 9:1-19 Daniel answer to prayer, Daniel chapter 10, 11 Daniel's prayer was unanswered for long time, until the act-Angle Michael got involved and wrestle with the principality in the air; got the answer and deliver it to Daniel. Daniel revealing prayer chapter 2:20-23 reveals Daniel's spiritual life which expresses absolute confidence in God's control over the Universes; Daniel clung to his faith in God even while living in the enemy nation that destroy Jerusalem Temple. Daniel's prayer also shows prayer of humility, praises and thanksgiving in the middle of affections and troubles. He praise and give thanks to God forgiven him the knowledge and wisdom understanding to interpret King Nebuchadnezzar dream.

Prayer for deliverance from trouble and worldly afflictions Psalm chapter 34

Prayer model of King Hezekiah's illness in the book of Isaiah chapter 38: 1-20 after Isaiah's vision to King Hezekiah, he did not give up; he wept bitterly and prayed ask God in prayer to remember his devotion, God had his prayer and sent prophet Isaiah back with a great message that he had added fifteen more years to his life.  Shows that God can change any effect through our prayer.

In the book of Jeremiah chapter 21:7 when King Zedekiah told prophet Jeremiah to pray to God on his behalf for a miracle God says No; because Judah need to change and come back to God first.

In the book of Matthew chapter 5:1-44 our Lord Jesus Christ teaches us about prayer. He told us to pray for our enemy, prayer for your persecutors, and he teaches about Fasting and prayer. He told us do not exercise revengeful spirit, we must follow God's commandments. Teaches us our Lord's Prayer:  Matthew 7:7-12, Our Lord's Prayer: 6:5-15; Luke 18:1-14 Prayer in the Garden of Gethsemane:  Matthew 26:36-46; Luke 22:40-46; Mark 14:32-42   Jesus teaches about the Parables of Widow and Unjust Judge: Luke 18:1-14 The Pharisee and Tax collector. Our Lord's Priestly Prayer for his disciples and all the Christians: John chapter 17:1-20 where he commissions the disciples to take over the gospel mission to the world this is our Lord Jesus Christ longest prayer.

Apostle Paul's prayer of thanksgiving romans 1:8-15; Ephesians 1:15-19; Paul's prayer for those who will read the Gospel Ephesians 3:4-21 Paul's prayer of thankfulness for Colossians  the book of Colossians chapter 1:3-14

Prayer of Apostle James in the book of James chapter 1:2-18 prayer for wisdom asking God for wisdom and faith during trials and tribulations; during difficult times to produce perseverance Joy and good quality life.

Teaches about how to overcome suffering in our life - The book of Romans 8:18-27 teaching that suffering bring out future glory; as well as life in the spirit.  Suffering brings future reward that outweigh all the present sufferings

# NEW YEAR PRAYER FOR ALL THE PEOPLE IN ALL THE NATIONS OF THE WORLD

*Let us PRAY:*

God the Father Almighty, Jesus Christ his only begotten Son, Holy Spirit one God;

You are the maker of heaven and earth sea and everything that dwells in it, we give you glory Jesus Christ the Son of God; full of truth and righteousness, we give you praise our Lord and Savior you are Worthy to be praised.  Lord Jesus Christ you the way the truth and the life, the Alpha and Omega, the beginning and the end, the first and the last, you're the great shepherd of the sheep, the chief shepherd and the good shepherd, all life dwell in you.  We pray for your mercy and protection every day of our life, keep us safe from violence, hatred, wars and rumors of wars, and bless us with your unending protection every day of our lives from all the violence, persecutions that is going on in all the nations of Earth. Protect your people, especially the police, the firemen, running around the city to save lives, save their own life our Lord.  Also, the News Media men, who are trying to get the news to us, the Army who are protecting our country, the children, the senior citizens, including men and women of all ages.   Protect us from Islamic Terrorists, The Taliban, Al Qaeda, ISIS, Boko haram in Nigeria and Hezbollah and all other terrorists in the world, in Sudan, in Kenya,

Somalia: turn them from evil to good, from hatred to love, from violent to peace, from wickedness to good.  They have turned the Holy Koran and the Muslim Religion into violence.  Deliver us our Lord let them know the truth and let the truth set them free. They are killing people in the Mosques and in the churches all over the Earth, destroying all the historical things of God.  Turn them around from enemies of God to the children of the ever-living and ever-loving God.  Deliver you people, the innocent people who are going through all forms of oppression, violence, murder and from sudden death.  Open Abu-Bakerdri's heart, mind, spirit and soul, the head of the ISIS to know that he is killing his own brothers and sisters and children every day.

We glorify God the Holy Spirit the giver of life, who proceeded from the Father and the Son. We are on Earth today because you breathe on us the breath of life; you blessed us with your Spirit and as a sustainer of life.  You sustain us, keep us safe, you provide for our needs and you fulfilled all our needs.  Lord Jesus Christ you are the God of all Nations the government is upon your shoulder.  You ordained the government of all the nations of this world; they are chosen by you, and they are your servants, let them know that they are serving you in all the areas of the governmental positions.

Thank you our Lord and Savior, all power dwell in you; you are the channels of blessings, from you all the goodness flows, you are the Prince of Peace, the Wonderful Counselor, our Prophet and our High Priest in heaven, the ascended God seated at the right hand of God, interceding for us at the right hand of God the Father. You are worthy of all our praises and thankfulness our God from the beginning of this year to the end.  You are the Prince of Peace.

Help us to start this New Year with your love, mercy, and great compassion.  O' God, most merciful Father, we give you praise for sending your only Son Jesus Christ, who took on Himself the form of a servant, and humbled Himself, becoming obedient even to death on the cross.  We give you praise and exalt Your Holy Name.  You made Jesus the Lord of All, and through Him, we know that whoever wants to be great must  first be a servant.  We give you praise for the ministry of all your churches in all the nations of this world.  Open the gates of heaven and let people of this world see your light unending.

In Your Great Matchless Holy Name, we pray, amen, amen, amen.

# SONG OF REJOICING IN THE LORD

*So send I you-- by grace made strong triumph o'er hosts of*

*Hell, o'er darkness, death, and sin, my name to bear and in that name to*

*Conquer-- so send I you, my victory to win.*

*So send I you--  to take to souls in bondage the Word of*

*truth that sets the captive free, to break the bonds of sin, to loose death's*

*Fetters – so send I you, to bring the lost to me.*

*Son send I you— my strength to know in weakness, my joy in*

*Grief, my perfect peace in Pain, to prove my power, my grace, my promised*

*Presence – so send I you, eternal fruit to gain.*

*So send I you— to bear my cross with patience, and then one*

*day with joy to lay it down, to hear my voice, well done, my faithful*

*servant— come, share my throne, my kingdom, and my crown*

*As the Father has sent me, so send I you.*

*Words: Margaret Clarkson, 1962 Music: .John W. Peterson, 1954*

# ABOUT THE AUTHOR

*Grace Dola Balogun graduated from Fordham University Graduate School of Religion and Religious Education with an M. A. in Religion and Religious Education. She has been a prayer mentor and advisor for many Christians of all denominations. Grace is also the author of Prayer the Source of Strength for Life, published in English and Spanish; and Spirit Power, Volumes One and Two, as well as the Cross and the Crucifixion, The Three Simple Solutions For World Peace, and Justification by Faith Alone in Christ Alone.*

*Visit Grace online at: graceligiliousbookspublishers.com*

## ORDER FORM

**TO ORDER YOUR COPY OF ANY BOOK:**

NAME: _______________________________________

ADDRESS: ___________________________________

TELEPHONE: _________________________________

FAX#:_______________________________________

MAIL: _______________________________________

QUANTITY: __________________________________

**MAIL TO:**

**Grace Religious Books Publishing & Distributors, Inc.**
**New York**
**248 Lombard Street 2nd Fl.**
**New Haven, CT 06513**

**ORDER ONLINE FROM: GRACE RELIGIOUS PUBLISHERS.COM**

**AMAZON, GOOGLE, SMARSHWORDS, BARNS & NOBLE, BOOKS A MILLION**

**INGRAMSPARK/LIGHTENING SOURCE ETC.**

# NOTES

# NOTES